ENCANTADO DREAMS

MORTALITY BITES SERIES

RAMY VANCE

KEEP EVOLVING STUDIOS

ENCANTADO DREAMS

CHAPTER ONE

*E*ven with five hundred years of immortality under my belt, I still couldn't apply lipstick right.

"Call me Isa," I said to my reflection, pressing my lips together. "No one calls me by my full name."

The girl who stared back at me widened her green eyes, adjusted one red curl back into her bun. The eyeshadow was too dark, the lips too red; after a year in this form, I still hadn't mastered the right shades for Irish coloring.

"I'll call you whatever you want," Aimee said, stepping into my line of vision in the mirror, "but if you make us late for class because you're pretending to be someone else again, I will play the Brazilian samba while you sleep."

I shuddered, turning toward her. "Not the samba. The drums are like a giant's footsteps on my eardrums."

She grabbed her backpack off her bed, slung it over one shoulder. "Then get your Gabbana-Coach-cinnamon-swirl whatever, and let's go."

"It's Dolce & Gabbana." I swiped a hand through the straps of my handbag. It was the perfect size for all my needs: textbooks, notebooks, my laptop, and even a makeup bag. I was starting to like fashion. "And I think it suits me, don't you?"

Of course, she thought the bag was a fake. How could I afford the real thing on a research assistant's wages? I hadn't told her—or anyone—about what I had stashed away in my savings account. Five hundred years was a long time to save.

Regardless, even if Aimee knew something about fashion, she would have been too kind to point out a fake.

Aimee crossed to the door, surveyed me as she opened it. "For class? Isabella, you could go in your pajamas and you'd be a knockout."

I offered her a faint smile as I passed through the door. She might have been right. After all, I knew what humans found "aesthetically pleasing," and this form was it. The youth, the red hair, the green eyes, the 0.7 hip-to-width ratio.

And yet. I stepped into the hallway, found myself staring at Justin Truly in profile. *Justin-Perfect-Truly,* I always thought when I saw him. Black-haired, blue-eyed, lithe as a jaguar and twice as muscular.

Jaguar, I thought automatically. *Kingdom: Animalia. Genus: Panthera. Class: Mammalia. Species: P. onca.*

"Uh, Isa?" Aimee said, stepping in front of me. "We have to get better about that staring thing. It's a little creepy."

"He's a jaguar," I murmured. Men like that were an endangered species.

Justin hadn't noticed me from where he stood, knocking on Katrina's door down the hall. No one answered. He straightened, and his eyes passed over Aimee and me. I waved, all my fingers moving separately.

He paused a half second, hitched his backpack up and started the opposite way down the hall.

"He didn't wave back," I said.

Aimee glanced the direction I was staring. "That wasn't a wave, Isa —you looked like you were casting a spell on him."

I smacked my forehead as Aimee laughed, turning us toward the stairwell. *"Merda,"* I said. "I think I'm losing my touch now that I'm mortal."

"It's fine. He's really good looking," she said as we started down the stairs. "But don't talk about him being a jaguar anymore, OK?"

"OK," I said. "Hey, wait up!"

Aimee was barreling down the stairs like a dervish, pulling on her hat and gloves. By the time we hit the first stairwell she was already fully suited up, only her eyes and nose visible. "We'll make it if we run," she called back to me, muffled through her scarf. "And not Isabella-running, either."

I was taking the steps a pair at a time, and I was breathless by the time we emerged onto the street. "Hey," I protested, "what does that mean?"

At that moment, the cold hit me like a wall. As a native Brazilian, I would never get used to Montreal winters.

"It means you're my best friend, but you run like a beached dolphin," Aimee said.

"Thank you." I set one hand to my chest.

She glanced back. "Why are you thanking me?"

"In my culture, it's an honor to be compared to a dolphin. They're the most intelligent mammals in the ocean, not to mention how my kind resembles—"

"Isa," she said. "Class. Stat." And before I could finish soapboxing, she struck down the plowed sidewalk toward the Liberal Arts building. I ran after, and as we careened past people walking down the sidewalk, I regretted wearing these black boots with their spindly heels.

Turns out, a pretty pair of heels does nothing for functionality.

"Porra!" I yelled, sliding on the ice.

It was only when I heard a "Woah," and felt a pair of hands catch me at the waist that I knew who had saved me.

My head turned, and I nearly melted into those blue eyes.

"You okay?" Justin-Perfect-Truly asked.

Aimee appeared next to us. "Sorry," she whispered to him, grabbing my hand and pulling me out of his arms. She always turned mousy and shy when we got outside. "We're going to be late for class."

And we were off again. "Curse you," I said. Suddenly I could have

5

cared less about English 101. You'd think since I was fluent in all the Romance languages (and a few others, to boot) I'd have tested out of the class. Turns out, if you're an Other, you don't get that option; as a sophomore, they had finally graduated me from English as a Second Language into the standard classes. "That could have been my chance at love."

"Trust me, Isa," Aimee said breathlessly, "you'll find love again."

I could only glance back to where Justin stood looking after us, both hands raised as though he'd been offered free samples at a Chinese restaurant in a mall food court.

He seemed awfully sad these days. Cute-sad, but sad nonetheless.

And as Aimee and I rushed into our English class and slipped into our seats, I couldn't help but wonder if that sadness had to do with Katrina Darling.

The auburn-haired, fashion dynamo had been missing since the start of the semester. Today, like every other day for the last three weeks, her seat in front of me remained as empty as ever.

↔

It wasn't any of my business what had happened to Katrina. We weren't friends, or even acquaintances. The most she'd ever said to me was "Thanks," when I passed her the syllabus on the first day of English 101.

And yet.

Maybe it was how boring our professor was, or the fact that I would get an A even if I happened to miss the next month of lectures —hey, I was octolingual—but her absence fascinated me.

As the professor called roll again, and "Katrina Darling?" came out of his mouth to no reply, I did that thing that encantados do.

I began to imagine her life. My hand went to the amulet around my neck, and I rubbed at the teardrop crystal as I envisioned her somewhere in Europe, riding low on the back of a teal vespa and chucking ninja stars at the legion of ghouls chasing her. Her auburn hair would have whipped out of its bun and she would have on a pair of those tall leather boots I'd seen her wearing once last semester—did she ever wear anything twice, for that matter?—and even on that vespa, she'd look cool.

I'd shifted into thousands of illusions in my time and never been that cool.

A pair of fingers snapped near my ear. "Isa," Aimee hissed. "You're up."

My eyes shot from Aimee to the professor, who stood with the tufts of his remaining hair blowing under the vent, one hand on his hip. "Ms. Ramirez?"

Merda. That was me. Part of that encantado thing: you get really, really hyperfocused on whatever you're fantasizing about—sort of like a human with ADHD.

"Coming." I tucked my amulet into my sweater and swept my report and USB drive off my desk. I was ready for this.

I made for the front of the classroom, and when I knelt in front of the computer, I struggled to fit the USB into the slot. I must have practiced a hundred times, but I was sweating through my sweater by the time it finally clicked in.

I sprang up to find twenty sets of half-lidded eyes staring back at me. If you think imitating humans for hundreds of years during your immortal life would prepare you for a 10-minute presentation in front of a classroom of mostly human college freshmen, you'd be wrong.

Very wrong.

I closed my eyes, took a deep breath as I indicated for our professor to dim the lights.

He stepped toward the door, made to close it on any late arrivals. But a hand caught the door just before it closed, and a set of extra-long nails tapped the wood.

Every pair of eyes turned to see who'd dared to arrive late. This professor was known to dress-down any students who thought they could barrel into his class after it had already started.

But this wasn't a student.

The door creaked slowly open to reveal an elderly woman in a long, black dress. She hadn't even worn a jacket; definitely not Canadian winter-wear. Her white hair had been left uncut and straggled almost to her hips. It framed a lined, unhappy face.

No—unhappy wasn't the right word. I'd spent so long studying faces and recreating them that I knew exactly how to read a person's face, especially if they were old.

This woman bore the face of a life lived bitterly. Frown lines framed her mouth, which pursed almost into lipless nonexistence. Two deep grooves sat between her eyebrows, what I'd often heard called "elevens."

Elevens were a sign of worry, of pain, of anxiety. And they had the side effect of permanently marring a face.

Even now, her eyebrows drew together as she surveyed the classroom. Emerald eyes, the whites bloodshot and yellowing, started at the back and swept over every face until she arrived at mine.

The scorn in those eyes practically leveled me. I set one hand on the rail along the bottom of the whiteboard.

"Can I help you?" the professor asked.

Her green eyes narrowed on me, studying my features. And the more I looked, the more they seemed familiar. But that couldn't be—I remembered every person I'd ever met. I was the Other equivalent of a "super recognizer," which meant I could remember anyone's face after seeing it once. Except I was beyond that. I had tens of thousands of faces in my memory.

And I didn't recognize this one.

But those eyes ... there was something about them.

The old woman didn't even acknowledge that the professor had spoken. She came toward me in a smooth motion, the hem of her dress kissing the ground almost as though she floated.

When she stopped, I had backed up against the whiteboard—I was going to have red marker residue all over my back after this—as she leaned toward me … and sniffed.

I lifted a finger. "Uh, excuse me."

The woman's hand came out, touched a tendril of my hair. She brought it to her nose and took one long, deep inhale. *"É você?"*

Had she just addressed me in Portuguese? If I'd heard her correctly, she had said, "Is it you?"

Even if she did speak my language, I really doubted I wanted to be the person she was looking for. I removed my hair from her grasp, and she allowed it to slide from between her fingertips. *"Desculpe,"* I said, *"nunca nos conhecemos."* Which translated to, "Sorry—we've never met."

Her eyes widened with recognition, like she'd seen someone she never expected to see again. I knew that look. Heck, I'd been responsible for that look before.

By now, the professor had stepped up behind the old woman and set both hands on her shoulders. She looked absolutely frail next to him, and his hands appeared enormous. "All right, let's figure out where you're supposed to be."

The woman's eyes hung on me, but she allowed herself to be turned toward the door. She flashed one last look around the classroom, her eyes darting toward me as she and the professor stepped outside.

"Isabella, we'll continue with your presentation in a minute," he said as the door swept shut behind him.

And as it clapped to, the whole class broke into nervous laughter. It was like they'd seen one of those guys in a hotdog suit come running through the lecture room and dash out the other side.

Except for me. My heart was beating like a bird in a cage.

CHAPTER TWO

The morning chill hadn't lifted, and Aimee and I walked slowly toward the dining hall.

"So," she began, "that was unusual."

"Understatement of the century." And I would know; I had been around for five centuries.

Even as we passed down the sidewalk packed with students going to and from classes, my eyes searched for that woman. Those green eyes were haunting me.

"Do you know her?" Aimee asked.

"How would I know her?"

"She sounded ... South American."

"That's kind of generalizing, Aimee. It's a big continent."

She shrugged. "Okay, whatever. You and she spoke in Portuguese, didn't you?"

I exhaled through my nose. "Yes." That woman had clearly been a native speaker. And she actually sounded like she might have been from Brazil.

"Maybe you knew her ... you know, before."

And by *before*, she meant when I was an immortal. Back before I had to burn time to shapeshift, and when years flowed through my fingers as simply as water over my dorsal fin.

Well, those rare times I actually took on my true form.

"I've never seen her face before," I said slowly. "But those eyes ..."

Aimee cast a curious look at me as she opened the door to the dining hall, and a wave of delicious hot air flowed over the both of us. Ahh, the wonders of modern heating. There were a few things I truly appreciated as a Brazilian in Canada, and this was in the top three.

Ahead of us, the morning crowd had assembled, most tables full of dull-eyed students in pajamas with bowls of sugar—what they called "cereal"—set before them. It was a miracle humans in the developed world lived as long as they did, given their day-to-day eating habits.

"The eyes? What do you mean?" Aimee asked.

"They were like ... " But I trailed off as my gut cinched. It had been seventy years, and I still couldn't even think about him without a physical reaction. And I really didn't want to talk about what had happened seventy years ago in the middle of the dining hall. So I just offered a faint smile. "They were like emeralds."

"I thought she was going to turn you into a pillar of salt with the way she was looking at you," Aimee said as we crossed to the tray dispenser. "Hey, isn't that—?"

We had caught sight of him at the same time, and I froze with the tray to my chest like a breastplate.

Justin Truly, and he was staring straight back at us over a giant pile of whipped cream. There might have been a waffle under there some-where, too.

"Yes," I whispered. "Is he looking at us or out the window?"

"I'd say he's looking at you, Isa."

I spun around, slamming my tray onto the rails. "No way. He's definitely looking at the pretty Montreal sky."

Aimee glanced outside. "The sky looks like a white coat that got trampled on by dirty boots. You should talk to him—he's alone."

"True." I thought about what she was suggesting, then I thought about who was suggesting it. "Wait a minute, aren't you Kat's friend? Why would you betray her like that?"

"We met a couple times. She was a little too aggressive for us to be friends. Not like you and me," Aimee said. "Kat's nice, but all's fair in love and war."

I grabbed an apple, set it on my tray. "I can't. He's with her."

She shrugged. "So? Doesn't mean he's a nun."

"Men can't be nuns."

She sighed. "It was a joke, Isa. Sometimes I think I should hang out with humans more often."

"Who would do your biology homework for you?" I flashed her a grin.

"Oh, that's it." She set both hands on my shoulders and turning me toward Justin. "Go figure out what genus and species he is, future biologist."

I yelped as she pushed me in his direction. "Hey, I haven't finished getting my food!"

Aimee grabbed a plate of salmon, set it on my tray. "Got you covered, fam."

Salmon was my absolute favorite. My gaze softened on Aimee; she really did know me.

I sighed, turned back to Justin. He had dug into his mountain of whipped cream, and even with his terrible dietary choices and down-cast eyes, I still couldn't help but find him dreamy.

I wanted to approach, but I felt frozen to the spot. How would Katrina walk over to him? Probably with a confident step and two arms slid tight around his waist, considering she hadn't been around for weeks.

And how would he react if he saw her? Those blue eyes would light up as I'd seen them do when she stepped out of our English class and he'd be waiting for her. His eyebrows would lift for a half-second —which signaled attraction and excitement among Homo sapiens— and he would stand, enfold her in his arms.

What if he could see her again? When the thought entered my mind, my hand flew to my chest, searching out my amulet. I pulled it from beneath my sweater, rubbed at the gem. I had seen Katrina often enough that I would only have to burn two months of my life to shift into her likeness.

A few months of life for a few hours of bliss? Sounded like a fair trade to me. We encantados really, really prized love, lust and everything in between.

I started toward the bathroom. I heard Aimee calling my name, but I didn't respond, heading straight for the single-stalled handicap bathroom. I needed the privacy, and it would only take me about ten minutes to change, so I wasn't *that* bad.

Just a little bad.

As I stepped into the bathroom, I shut the door and locked it. When I turned, my redheaded visage stared back at me.

"Stop judging me," I said. The face who stared back had actually been a young woman I'd seen traveling in Rio, shortly before I'd flown to Montreal. And she had looked so...glamorous, so glorious. I'd thought, there's the perfect person for me to be.

There's the person who'll change everything.

But soon after I'd arrived at McGill, all that gloriousness had fallen away. Now she only looked pallid and judgmental under the fluorescent light. That look reminded me of how *he* had stared at me, all those decades ago.

I closed my eyes, gripping my amulet. I envisioned Katrina Darling: the brown-blonde hair, her heart of a face, the green eyes. And as I did, a tremor of power passed through me.

Magic. It had been so long, just a taste of it felt immense.

After a moment, it surged in me, filling my body like carbonate. First it slipped into my bones, cracking them with painful abruptness. I had to be shorter. I had to be finer-boned. Even my facial structure had to change.

I gritted through it all, my eyes firmly shut. Back before the gods left—when I could use magic as freely as I could breathe air—I hadn't thought anything of shifting into a new form. Now I could feel the hours rolling off the end of my life. The whole process had become a little scary.

But, how does the saying go? Fashion hurts.

Shutter flashes of Katrina Darling passed through my mind: the back of her perfectly groomed head in English class, the sight of her walking through campus, how she smiled, how she frowned, how she contemplated.

Then came the muscles. They refitted themselves to my new frame, reshaping slender and lithe. The vocal cords adjusted to create the cadences of her speech.

I hadn't expected everything to shrink so much. Katrina Darling was even smaller than my old form, which wasn't very large to begin with. For some reason, I'd always thought she was … bigger than that. And I wasn't referring to adipose tissue. Her presence in class, when she spoke, had always made her seem larger than the body she occupied.

And I realized, mid-shift, that she didn't necessarily see herself as limited by her size. She was who she was.

When I opened my eyes in the handicapped stall, I flinched. There she was, watching me. It was almost as though Katrina Darling had snuck in while I was shifting and was staring me down.

When I lived in Brazil, we encantados had always called ourselves artists. We even had a test by which we judged our shapeshifting: if we saw our own reflection and felt, for a heart-stopping moment, that we had been found out by the person we were imitating, we had succeeded. We had made a person come to life.

I had passed that test many times, but today, I had captured Katrina Darling more acutely than perhaps any shift I'd attempted before. The hair, the face, everything.

Maybe it was the knowledge of my own impermanence, that I was sacrificing two months of my life to create this portrait of a woman. Or maybe it was the inspiration. The hair, the face, everything.

I ticked some fake dust off the shoulder of my sweater—which was a little big on me now—and grinned.

The door handle jostled, and a knock followed.

"Be just a minute," I called, and jerked my head around to survey the empty stall. It was like she had spoken over my shoulder.

When I opened the door, a young woman in a wheelchair idled a few feet off. She offered me a slant-eyed look, surveying my perfectly able body.

My first instinct was to apologize, but I suppressed it. Would Katrina apologize? She didn't ever seem sorry for anything. But it was right to be sorry for taking up the handicapped bathroom when I didn't legitimately need it.

Something the campus therapist for Others had suggested during our last session came to mind. Instead of apologizing, thank people. But what should I thank her for?

Anxiety—the familiar teeter-totter between my old personality and this new one I still wore like a costume—swelled in me like a fist gripping my heart. Maybe this had been a mistake, becoming Katrina. My assertiveness was melting before I'd even left the bathroom.

I hovered for a few seconds in front of the door until she began rolling her chair forward. "Are you done?" she said. "I really have to go."

I blinked hard, stepped aside. "Yes, I'm done. Thank you for being patient with me."

I didn't know if that was what Katrina would have said, but it was what felt right in the moment. It felt right for me.

She glanced up at me for a second, and the ghost of a smile touched her lips. "I like your bag," she said, and then she rolled past me into the bathroom.

I grinned after her. *Score one for the Dolce Gabbana bag.* That sounded like something she might say.

When I walked back into the dining hall, no one seemed to notice at first. After all, I just looked like your typical (super cute) college freshman. It wasn't until I'd crossed in amongst the tables that I spotted Aimee, sitting alone with two trays. One was mine, the salmon now cold on the plate. I felt a pang of guilt, but I'd apologize to her later for skipping out.

As I passed her, she lifted her eyes, paused with a big spoonful of pudding in her mouth. *"Ka-sriba?"*

I pretended I hadn't heard her. Instead, I beelined for the table where Justin sat. He'd managed to plow through about half of that pile of whipped cream, and I smirked as I leaned against the table, one hand set flat on its surface.

"That's sweet, lover." I reached down, swept up a fingerful and set it between my lips. "You got a double portion for me."

↔

In my years as an encantado, I've experienced a lot of adoring gazes. Men and women alike have looked at me like I'm their goddess, the heroine of their own personal fairy tale.

And for a time, I was. Always for a time. I could inspire that adoration within a few days, and I could even make it last weeks or months. But the illusion always faded, the lust rarely passing into something deeper, truer. It might have had something to do with showing them my real form, or it might have been an inevitability.

Despite it all, the thrill of that adoring gaze never became less potent.

But that wasn't the look Justin gave me when his eyes rose to my face. I registered shock in his raised eyebrows and open mouth. Then a dash of confusion, the eyebrows pulling together to form those *elevens* I mentioned earlier.

"Kat?"

"In the flesh." I tilted my head with a smile.

For a half-second, his eyes softened into wrought affection, and he stood, came around the table and pulled me into his arms. "What are you doing here? Where have you been?"

I melted into his tight embrace, ran my hands along the hard muscle of his torso and back. GoneGods be true, the muscles. And the warmth—he was impossibly warm, like a furnace.

When he kissed the top of my head and smelled my hair, it felt better than I'd ever imagined, and I had imagined it being pretty awesome. Definitely worth the burnt time.

"Good to see you, too," I murmured into his chest.

After a moment, he stepped back, both hands on my arms. That furrow returned to his eyebrows, and then he got upset.

"That's what you have to say after all this time? 'Good to see you?' Kat, I've been freaking out. You haven't been in your classes, you haven't been on campus, you haven't responded to my emails. Your phone has been off. You just disappeared, and you never even called or texted or sent me a single word to let me know you hadn't died."

Really, Kat? I thought. Then, *Who am I to judge Kat's choices?* But she did leave me in a tight spot.

My mouth opened, but I didn't know what to say. Blood rushed in my ears, my heart like a drumbeat, and my brain's circuitry felt completely inefficient, sparking in all the wrong places.

"I ..." I began.

But before I could answer, I was saved by the sounds of shattering glass and screaming students as the biggest wolf I'd ever seen in my five hundred years burst into the dining hall.

CHAPTER THREE

*J*ustin and I stared, both frozen, at the creature that had just exploded through a pane of glass and stood bristled and red-eyed at the front of the dining hall.

Most of the half-asleep students took a second longer than normal people would to respond, and then the first scream broke out. With that, more pairs of checkered pajamas than I've ever seen at once were rushing toward the exits.

Instead of fleeing like the others, Justin only grabbed my hand. "What the hell is that?"

I squinted at the creature. It resembled a wolf, but many times as large; its spine probably cleared ten feet at the crest. And its eyes glowed such a fiery red, it reminded me more of a hellhound, or...

"Lobisomem," I whispered, and immediately ducked us under the dining table. We were at the back of the room—trapped, without any nearby exits—and anyone who could had already taken off through a side door or scrambled into one of the hallway.

Which left just a few people huddling under tables—and me and Justin.

Justin turned to me. "What did you say?"

I looked over at his beautiful, ignorant face. "It's death. We need to get out of here."

He shook his head. "If it's death, we need to help these people. You and I need to fight it."

"We can't fight—" I began, and stopped sudden. *You and I,* he'd said, like this was a familiar thing. "What do you mean, 'fight it?' "

"You know, like as Cherub." He mimed sliding a mask over his face and stabbing the air with a knife. "Well, mostly you fighting it and me cheering you on."

I stared at him. Katrina Darling was that girl I'd seen in the cherub mask? Over the past few months we'd had some crazy things happen on campus, most involving monsters, and during one of those events I'd been walking through campus when I saw a girl in a cherub mask rush by with a pack of … superheroes behind her.

As in, *Avengers*-style, fireball-shooting people in costumes and capes.

So Kat wasn't a normal college freshman, and that wasn't just because of her style and her perfectly coiffed hair.

A low, rumbling growl emanated from the front of the dining hall, and from beneath the table, I could see that the creature—could it really be a lobisomem?—was slowly crossing in amongst the tables.

And it seemed to be sniffing. I heard the distinct sound of a snout sucking in air, tasting scents.

Fear rose up my spine like ice water. What was it scenting for?

The *lobisomem* was a creature of South American lore, most popular in children's stories told after nightfall. Most humans didn't believe it was real—and I hadn't, either—but a single detail of the stories I'd heard stood out to me as too great a coincidence.

They were summoned creatures, called into this plane to bring death to anyone their summoner marked as prey. And lobisomem were singularly capable when it came to scenting magic.

Or more specifically, the *use* of magic. They could smell it from a hundred miles.

I had used magic just a few minutes ago. And my illusions were sustained by it. But this lobisomem was something more, something different than the stories I'd heard ... This one seemed to interfere with my magic. I stared down at my hands, terrified.

"What is it, Kat?" Justin asked.

My gaze lifted to him. "Do I look different to you?"

Another growl issued from the far end of the hall—it was near the bathroom now—followed by more screams and pounding feet.

"This isn't really the time, babe," Justin said.

Putting aside the fact he'd called me "babe," which made my heart beat faster than it already had been, I scooted closer to him. "This thing is too dangerous for us to fight here," I breathed into his ear. "We need to get out of this building, and maybe we can lure it away from the other students."

He nodded. "Good call. How?"

A trash can fell over with a loud clang, and I flashed a glance over my shoulder toward the hallway. The creature's tail disappeared around the corner. Was he following the scent of my magic? "We run," I said, pushing Justin out from under the table.

We bolted for the front door of the dining hall, though I moved awkwardly in my boots. My feet were smaller than they had been before, which didn't couple well with heels.

I stumbled, and Justin caught me. (*What a hunk*, I thought for the briefest of infatuated moments.) The closest exit was the floor-to-ceiling window the wolf had crashed in through, and Justin ran us straight out through it, our feet crunching over the broken glass.

That was a mistake. As soon as we ran over that glass, a snarl sounded from down the hallway. We spun right and tore down the sidewalk, and the wolf of Amazonian legend blasted out of the dining hall after us.

It skidded to a stop, and I thought maybe we'd fit in with all the other students running for their lives. But then it let a howl so loud they must have heard it throughout the entire province, and the wolf clawed the pavement with gravel-crunching power as it leapt into motion after us.

Lobisomem was on the hunt now.

↔

"Which way?" Justin yelled.

"Here." I hooked a right and took us down a narrow alley. The creature wouldn't be slender enough to follow us through here—or so I'd thought.

Ten seconds later, the ground rumbled as it leapt onto the roof of the building to our right, and I heard the pounding of its paws as it ran behind us … twenty feet up.

I ventured a glance up and back, spotted those red eyes staring back down at me, the lips curled into a snarl. Those canines were as long as my newly reshaped forearm.

"Don't look up," I breathed, already totally winded.

"I hadn't planned on it." To his credit, Justin seemed to be fine when it came to lung capacity. He was an athlete, after all. He pointed some twenty feet ahead of us, where a door led off into a building. "Underground?"

He was pointing to an entrance to Montreal's underground mall and tunnels, which ran throughout the campus and the city. I had an acute map of them in my head because, in my Brazilian hatred of the cold, I'd used them all the time.

The lobisomem wouldn't be able to get down the narrow stairwell, and even if he managed to, navigating that space would definitely slow it down.

"Underground," I agreed.

We darted left, our shoes tapping hard on the stairs as we plunged down the passageway. A woman carrying a shopping bag in each hand trudged up the steps in the opposite direction, and I yelled, "You'll want to use a different exit!" as we barreled by.

We hit the tiled floor at a run, and we didn't slow. Behind us, a massive thud sounded as the wolf presumably leapt down into the alley. The woman we'd passed let out a scream, and I glanced over my shoulder.

She had dropped her bags and was careening back down the way she'd come. Behind her, the creature's head and forepaws were trying to press inside the entryway to the stairwell. But he was stuck. He let a frustrated howl conveying as much, and the sheer loudness of it made me clap my hands over my ears as we ran past stores and shops.

We took the first turn we saw, which led us left and deeper into the tunnels. "I think … we're safe," I panted.

Justin wouldn't let go of my hand, and he kept pulling me on. "If a semester of fighting monsters and nasty Others with you has taught me anything, it's that you should never stop moving when you think you're safe."

"Then you'll have to go on without me," I said, gasping for breath. I stumbled, and he finally ducked us into a lingerie shop. We nearly knocked over a scantily clad mannequin as we tumbled in, and the attendant—half-folded panties in hand—stared at us with wide eyes.

"It's her birthday," Justin said, navigating us past the attendant, "and she's really excited to get her present."

I raised a hand as we passed, my cheeks about ten degrees hotter than the rest of me, and the attendant offered a wan smile before she resumed folding.

When we got into the back, we stood next to a rack of teddies and, breathing hard, stared at the store's entrance. Far off, I could hear the howling and some vague screams. But they didn't seem to be getting any closer.

"Is it still coming?" Justin whispered.

"Maybe?"

As soon as I'd said it, the howling stopped. We waited in a held-breath stasis for four or five minutes, but everything seemed to have returned to normal. Well, more or less.

There was still this fact: a creature of Amazonian legend had appeared in Montreal, and had chased me across the campus and into a Victoria's Secret.

Justin turned to me, and I to him. And before I could say anything, he wrapped his arms around me and pressed me into a kiss so delicious my thoughts slipped back into Portuguese.

After a minute or an hour or a day, a voice filtered in. "Can I help you two with anything?"

Filho da puta.

Justin pulled away with a soft laugh. "No, thanks."

But I just stayed right where I was, my lips parted. That had been the best kiss of my long, long life. (A little hyperbolic, sure, but we encantado live in the moment.) My eyes slowly drifted to the attendant, whom I might have burnt to the ground if my gaze were capable of such a thing.

"I'm afraid you'll have to save that for elsewhere." She winked at us as she turned away.

"Well," he said, lowering his hands to hold mine, "I think we're safe to leave."

I nodded, and we walked together out of the store and through one of the far exits. In the tunnels we saw the remnants of the lobisomem's presence—a candy display knocked over, someone's coat dropped as they fled—but an attendant was already righting the display, and people were back to their shopping.

No screams, no howling. How quickly mortal terror shifted back into mid-morning errands.

"Do you think we ought to go back?" I asked.

Justin shot me a look. "Why?"

"We could see what's up—maybe it's still stuck in the stairwell."

"Like a dog in a kitty door?"

I suppressed a smile. "I guess."

"As funny as that would be, absolutely not."

"I thought you wanted to fight it."

"Yeah, when we were cornered," Justin said. "But that was only because we had no other option. Look at me, Kat—what would I fight with, anyway?"

I'll admit it: I took the opportunity to look him over before I said, "Point taken." We headed in the opposite direction down the tunnel and climbed another set of stairs leading back up to the city.

When we came into the daylight, I fully expected my face to be the recipient of two sets of angry claws, but nothing hit me except a wave of brittle cold.

Out here, the day went on, and the world went on. And so did we, Justin and Katrina, except we walked much faster than two lovers normally would. We walked like we were being followed.

"Your place?" he asked.

I gritted my teeth, shook my head. We definitely weren't going there. "Can we go to yours?"

"Sure, it's just that you don't usually like to come to the O³ house…"

"It's fine."

"Okay." He took the lead. "What did you call that thing? Lobo?"

"Lobisomem," I said, scanning ahead of us and behind. Everything still seemed normal, but wolves weren't loud creatures … until they were. They were quiet predators when they needed to be. "It's a creature of South American legend. A hunter."

"How do you know that?"

My eyes flicked to him. Maybe Kat shouldn't know such things. "The Other Studies Library," I said. "I've been on a creatures of South American lore kick lately."

"Of course you have," he said. "Wait, but when did you get back to Montreal?"

"I mean, I was on a kick before winter break," I corrected. The more we talked, the more things seemed to be gumming up. Names, dates, places, people. I began to realize how little I actually knew about Katrina Darling. If only he'd asked me what color my hair was, or what desk I sat at in English 101. But he wasn't going for the easy questions.

So I did something I had been wanting to do for months. I threw my arms around Justin, pressed my whole body to his, and pulled his face down. When our lips met, I parted his with my tongue, and I felt his body stiffen before it relaxed into mine.

I had felt this before. Many times. During my centuries of immortality I had fallen in love with hundreds of men, and they with me. Or at least, most had fallen into an all-encompassing passion with me.

I was always a beautiful young woman. It was the gender I associated myself with, as all encantado are biologically female. You see, legend and lore have it wrong about us … encantado have never been male. That's our blessing, our curse: we're the superior gender, but we can't reproduce with male encantado because there are none, and human men can't impregnate us, either.

We're functionally barren.

But that fact has never made me any less desirous of men.

While some among us didn't prefer them, I always had. Oh, how I preferred them. There's a reason Michelangelo sculpted David. The human male form, properly developed and cared for, is unmatched.

The other part of the encantado curse is our predisposition for obsession. Sometimes—once every few decades—we'll see a man, and then we won't be able to see any other man until we've been with that one. And by "been with," I don't just mean in the physical sense. I mean the whole shebang: physically, emotionally, spiritually.

Often, we aren't able to break that obsession until that man dies. It's more or less how humans define "love," and it had happened to me a dozen times over hundreds of years, though never since the gods had left.

Not until now. For me, Justin Truly was one of those men.

When I pulled away, he stared at me wide-eyed.

"Take me back to your place," I whispered.

CHAPTER FOUR

I didn't see any of what we passed on the way into the O³ house. There might have been other rooms, and there might have been stairs. I also remembered something about a door he pushed me up against on our way into his bedroom.

And there also might have been a killer wolf still out there, hunting the two of us. But for the next hour, we didn't properly exist in Montreal. We occupied a half-place where I only knew touch and taste and smell, and all of it felt like too much and not enough.

Which is to say, I nearly killed the man.

Afterward, he lay sprawled across his bed, panting. "You ..."

I smiled, propping myself on my elbow. One finger traced figure eights on his chest. "Me?"

"Those things you did," he said, half-delirious. "The part with the tongue and the earlobe. And then you bit me." He lifted his head to inspect his shoulder.

"You seemed to like it."

The blue eyes turned to me. "Kat, that was ... unreal. It was like you, but not you."

My stomach flipped, and I said nothing. I placed a delicate kiss on his lips before I lay back on the pillow and cast my eyes around his bedroom. Neat, orderly, if not a bit gender-stereotypical: lots of deep blues and dark-stained wooden furniture and some football awards gleaming off the walls.

"Where did you learn those moves?" he persisted.

"A lady never reveals her secrets." But the truth was: he wouldn't like the answer. Men didn't often like knowing that their woman had gained her intimate knowledge elsewhere, from another.

At least, not the men I've loved.

I sat up to pull on my panties and top. Beside me, a window streamed in the last dregs of light. It would be nighttime soon. If there was one thing I remembered from the legend of the lobisomem, it was that the night was its habitat. Prime time for hunting.

Justin's hand slipped it around my waist, pulled me back toward him. I shrieked as I slid up against his body and he pressed my head to his chest. "I want you right here."

I conformed myself to the shape of him, pressing my head into the hollow of his shoulder. "Right here is pretty nice."

He stroked my shoulder. "That thing is still out there."

"It is."

"What are we going to do about it?"

"I don't know yet," I said. And I honestly didn't. All I wanted to do was enjoy Justin, to forget that anything existed outside the frame of this bed. It was immature, irresponsible, and I didn't care.

So I did the thing that makes all men forget whatever it was they were talking about. And when I did it, Justin's eyebrows rose, he turned his face to me, and we sank—or slid, or glided—into the second show of the evening.

Maybe, I thought, *just maybe it'll disappear.* Maybe the lobisomem had been unsummoned. Maybe I wouldn't have to deal with any of this, and Justin and I could just forget about it all.

That was the thought I fell asleep with, while outside the moon shone like a gleaming quarter over our heads.

↔

. . .

In the morning, Justin and I did the most couple-y thing you could think of: I gave him my "new" phone number, and then we walked arm-in-arm to the coffee shop. On the way, he stopped us in front of a poster. Beneath the obnoxiously massive World Government symbol, it read:

The World Army wants you!

Think you have what it takes to train with humanity's best?

Come find out at our recruitment session at McGill's Fitness Center — 5pm this Thursday.

"Ugh," I said automatically. The World Army—the encapsulation of just about everything that was wrong with this world. They were so Otherist it wasn't even funny. It was scary, actually.

"Ugh?" Justin glanced at me.

Then I remembered: I wasn't Isabella. I was Katrina Darling, who might be of a different opinion about the whole thing. I waved a hand. "Nothing. I got a hair in my mouth."

"What do you think about me joining this?" Justin pointed at the poster. "I could be more useful to you."

Useful to me? I didn't know what he meant by that, but Katrina seemed like a tough girl. She probably liked her men rough and tumble.

"I don't know much about it," I said. "But if it would make you stronger, why not?"

"OK." He gave the poster another once-over. "Maybe I'll go to the session."

At the cafe, we drank from tiny cups while admiring each other from either end of a small, wrought iron table.

"You drink coffee now." Justin eyed my pure shot of espresso. "And not watered down, either."

"Turns out college brings on a lot of vices," I said, taking a short sip. "What have you been up to over the break?"

"I was home with my parents." His shoulders rounded a little; this clearly made him uncomfortable. "I was pretty sad for a while, though I found ways to distract myself."

I paused with my cup half-raised. "Sad?"

"About us. The way we fought before break." His hand reached out to me. "I'm so glad we've fixed things, Kat. I'm sorry about what happened with dybbuk, for my part in all of it."

Dybbuk. I had never heard of such a person—or such an ugly name. Had Justin cheated on Kat? I was irate on her behalf (even if I was the one with whom he was technically cheating now. Sort of). "Oh," I said. He waited for me to say more, so I added, "I accept your apology."

This made him smile. "I'm happy with you. It feels like things are different between us—you're asking me more questions and listening to my answers more closely. You're more forgiving."

I set my hand over his. "That's because I care about you."

I didn't know if he and Katrina had exchanged the L-word; I hadn't heard him say it to me yet. But I did care about Justin, and I wanted to hear what he had to say about things.

I might have been bound to obsession by my encantado nature, but that didn't mean I couldn't recognize a good man when I saw one. And the truth was, every time I'd seen him over the past five months, he had been doing something decent, even if it was just giving his attention to the person he was with.

He had grown on me in the way most good things do: in small, incremental moments. Even if he hadn't been aware of those moments.

He rubbed his thumb over my knuckles and a shiver went up my arm. The smallest inkling came to me that he might actually like Isabella—me—even if I didn't look like Katrina Darling.

"The way you handled that creature yesterday," he said, "it made me so proud of you."

I leaned close. "You mean the lobisomem?"

He touched my nose with one finger. "Yes, I mean the lobisomem."

A smile touched my lips, then disappeared. "But all I did was run."

"You led it out of the dining hall, away from all those students. And you had the brilliant thought of making for the underground, which saved both our bacons. You're so brave. It's the reason I fell for you."

This was all very sweet, but my gut cinched. He liked Kat because she was brave, which was the opposite of how I'd spent pretty much my entire immortal and mortal life operating.

Subterfuge. Illusions. Hiding. Avoiding confrontation. Those were my bread and butter.

Yesterday, all I had done was run away from that creature. And if it showed up now, I would do it again. I would hide, hope all my problems would disappear while I kept my head down.

You could call me Isabella "Avoidance" Ramirez.

Justin was studying me. "What's wrong?"

I refocused on the man at hand. "You fell for me because I'm brave?"

"And because you're cute. But that was just what turned my head. It's who you are that I care about."

I sighed, closing my eyes. *"Merda."*

"What did you say?"

Right—Kat probably didn't know Portuguese. "Nothing." I pulled my hand from under his, shame enveloping me like a blanket. Another thing about encantados: we're often driven by emotion, by the moment.

And in this moment, I felt terrible. He didn't deserve the Katrina Darling currently sitting across from him. He deserved better—a woman who would step to the plate when she was tested.

And all of this—the trickery, the illusion—suddenly felt very wrong, and very stupid of me.

I'd opened my mouth to tell him as much when a hand slapped down in the center of our little table, sending our cups toppling. We both jerked back as coffee landed in our laps.

Around us, the cafe went silent. Every face turned.

The hand between Justin and me didn't move, its long fingernails biting into the tablecloth. The back of that hand had lost some of its pigmentation to age, the coloring separating into light and dark spots pressing into wrinkles upon wrinkles.

I knew that hand. My eyes followed it to the wrist and up the arm it belonged to, finally landing on the face of the old woman who'd walked into my English class yesterday.

"Eu sabia que era você," she whispered, so small and shrunken she barely rose higher than me when I was seated.

But she was terrifying nonetheless. She stared right at me, those green eyes boring into mine, and I thought again how familiar they were just before she raised an enormous claw and drew it down my arm as delicately as if she were opening an envelope.

↔

A line of red blood emerged where the old woman's claw had ripped through my white shirt and into my skin. It wasn't a deep cut, but that didn't stop her from straightening and pointing the red-tipped end of the claw at my face.

"A maldição da minha família volta para você," she growled with triumph. Which meant, "The curse on my family comes back to you."

And then, before I or Justin or anyone else thought to react, she turned and swept out of the cafe and onto the street, her white hair and dress floating behind her.

For his part, Justin was too absorbed by the hot coffee all over his pants. When he looked back up at me, I'd already thrown my hand over the cut on my arm and stood from my seat.

"Kat," he said, then his brow furrowed. "Hey, you're looking kind of … pink."

My breath caught. The other patrons were staring at us—at me. And the old woman was gone through the double doors. No one had seen her—not Justin, not the barista at the counter, not the other people sitting around us.

"The curse," she had said. Coming from a superstitious culture, I was acutely familiar with curses—we encantado end up cursed often.

Over five hundred years I'd been called all sorts of names, and I was used to it. I mean, I never *enjoyed* being cursed, but I empathized with those left behind when a man chose to run away with an encantado.

And by that, I mean: I never blamed them.

But sometimes they weren't just idle curses. On occasion, people who have been so severely wronged curse themselves with all sorts of nasties: they vow never to die, never to find love. They do this as an exchange, because the flipside of that curse is that they gain certain ... well, for lack of a better word, powers.

And this old woman's power was the Mark of the Huntress.

I'd seen it before. The Mark of the Huntress granted the cursed the ability to hunt their prey. When that happened, the focus of the cursed person's hatred could easily shroud them from the sight of others. As a result, the cursed often appeared as a shadow to everyone else— except the one marked. You know, just to freak them out.

And I was the one marked.

"I got coffee all over me," I said. "I have to nip to the bathroom."

Justin stood and said something, but I was already halfway through the cafe, weaving my way past tables and all the eyes staring at my arm, which was starting to sting a little.

Not just sting—burn.

I stepped into a bathroom covered in a patchwork of faux-sophisticate art, a wallpaper of sketches and pithy quotes crafted over the years by an assortment of McGill's students.

In the half-light, I lifted my hand from my arm, and a small puff of white smoke rose from the cut.

Yes, that's right: I emitted smoke.

I swallowed, glanced up at my reflection in the circular mirror. If I hadn't been ready for something wild, I might have shrieked at my own appearance.

I looked like Katrina Darling if her mom had mated with a pink fish. That is to say, I had scales instead of smooth cheeks, and my entire body was quickly changing into another form.

My form. The one I never wanted to see again.

Smoke was still rising from the cut on my arm, evaporating into

32

the air around me. As I watched it go, I realized it wasn't your typical smoke. It had an almost airy, luminous quality about it, and a particular scent.

Understanding hit me all at once, and I had to sit on the porcelain toilet with my face in my hands.

My magic was being nullified, dispersing off my body and into the air. I was quickly losing the illusion I had burnt two months of my life to take on, and I didn't know if that was temporary or forever.

I grabbed some toilet paper off the roll, dabbed at the cut. It wasn't bleeding, precisely—more like my magical essence was seeping out of it in a clear line. That wasn't the color of encantado blood—ours was more a hot pink—but the color of my magic.

I pressed the toilet paper to the cut. That Brazilian woman had done this with the claw she'd been carrying. I squeezed my eyes shut, trying to render it in my mind. It had been about a foot in length, which meant the creature it once belonged to was big. Enormous.

And it was curved and razor-sharp, which meant it wasn't just for clawing and gripping—it was for ripping, tearing. Killing.

My eyes opened, and I stared at one of the pithy sayings written on the wall across from me: *When someone shows you who they are, believe them.*

A knock sounded on the door. "Kat? It's Justin."

I shot up from the toilet, and would have spun back to the mirror if I didn't flop over onto the floor. I gasped, which came out squeakier than I'd hoped. When I glanced down, a pink fish tail stared back at me.

I'd lost my legs.

CHAPTER FIVE

*I*n Brazil, some consider the encantado an enchantress. Some consider her mesmerizing, and they desire to see one as much as they fear it, for she is considered irresistible.

Here's the thing about those dreams: they're an illusion. An illusion of a young, beautiful woman.

The true encantado, without pretense or facade, will flop around on the bathroom floor of a coffee shop in Montreal like Darryl Hannah in *Splash*, but she will not be so graceful, nor so charming.

Because the true encantado form is something between a mermaid and a dolphin, with a mermaid's general shape—fishlike lower body, human upper body—and a dolphin's voice. A *pink* dolphin's voice. Except we're much more intelligent—no insult to dolphins, who tend to be kinder.

"One second!" I tried to call, but a series of squeaks came out between my rows of serrated teeth.

Oh yeah—I forgot about the serrated teeth.

All in all, we're the bizarro mermaids. The ones from your nightmares.

"Kat?" Justin called through the door. "What was that noise?"

That claw had completely nullified my magic; every bit of my illusion had left me, and while I was still Isabella Ramirez on the inside, if Justin were to walk into this bathroom right now, he wouldn't see anyone he recognized.

He would only see a creature. A fish.

Ugly. Abhorrent. A fearful, strange thing.

He kept knocking, saying Kat's name. And I knew, with a leap of the heart, that he wouldn't just leave. He wouldn't go until he felt everything was set right, until he heard Kat's voice saying, "It's OK, Justin. I'm OK."

What a thing, to have someone care about you like that.

I stilled on the floor. If only I could regain her voice, I could tell him everything was OK, that I needed more time. I closed my eyes, willing my magic to work. After I had assumed an illusion once, I could shift between forms almost seamlessly, only burning a second or two of my life to bring back a previous illusion.

I tried to bring back Katrina. Normally I'd feel the magic working, flitting over me like a static breeze, but I felt a whole lot of nothing.

And now there was someone else in the hallway—a young woman's voice. One of the baristas, asking Justin if everything was all right with me. She offered to get a key and open the door.

I wanted to cry, "No!" but it would have only produced another squeak.

So I squeezed my eyes shut harder, tensing my entire body. This time the magic came leaking out, drop by drop, like water from a faucet.

Goddess Yemoja! My magic was slowly returning.

I heard the barista's keyring jangling outside the door, and I tested my voice. "Hey!"

The keys paused. "Kat?" came Justin's voice. "You sound ... strange."

Well, I might have been higher-pitched, but at least I was forming words. "I'm fine. I just need a few more minutes," I said. "This coffee is really hard to get out of white cotton."

"I'll just wait at the table for you, then."

The magic was leaking out a little faster now, but not fast enough for me to finish the illusion while we were talking. Not nearly fast enough.

"No—I don't want to keep you waiting. Let's just meet up later, OK?"

"It's fine. I don't mind waiting, Kat. It's been so long since I've seen you."

"Just go," I pleaded. "I'll find you in an hour or two."

"I'll be in class in an hour—"

"Then I'll find you later tonight at the house!" I snapped.

He didn't answer right away, and I wanted to let him know that this wasn't me—I wasn't the angry type. These were just extenuating, fishlike circumstances, and I really couldn't have him seeing me in this state.

But I didn't say any of those things. I could sense Justin debating what to do while I lay on the floor in a writhing ball of anxiety and shame. In the end, he only said, "OK, Kat. See you later." And I heard the door close behind him. I guess their fight had left Justin wary of outright disobeying her. Whatever happened had happened because he ignored her boundaries or demands.

As much as I wanted to yell out for him to come back, what was done was done. He was gone, and I had successfully managed to alienate the one person I wanted to be near.

↔

Twenty minutes later, after a great deal of flopping and cursing, Katrina Darling finally emerged from the bathroom. Except this Katrina Darling looked like hell. Her shirt had a tear, her hair was out of place, and she had a hollow-eyed look like she'd seen some things.

At least I'd been able to get the illusion back.

When I emerged from the hallway, I peered around the cafe. The place looked exactly as it had when Justin and I arrived, which was to say, no old Brazilian women with claws.

And then the thought struck me: *Brazilian.* That woman had spoken Portuguese and she'd had the Mark of the Huntress. That particular curse was unique to just a few villages of the Amazon rainforest, and provided exceptional power. But more importantly, she was of *my* culture, and perhaps of my past.

I hurried out of the cafe and headed straight for my dorm. Aimee would be in right now, taking her midday nap—or at least, she would be if she had recovered from the whole giant wolf attack.

On that note, I thought as I came into the stairwell and started climbing, I hadn't checked on her after everything had happened in the dining hall. Instead, I had gone straight to Justin's place and forgotten about my roommate entirely.

I made a face; I was being a terrible best friend.

"Please be OK, please be OK," I whispered as I emerged into our hallway and yanked out my room key from my bag. I didn't hear anything on the other side of the door.

When I opened the dorm room door, I let a sigh. Aimee was there in bed, sleeping. She rolled over when I came in, bleary eyes opening. "Hey..." Then she sat up with a suddenness that made me stop hard. "Katrina?"

Right—I hadn't told her about my new illusion.

"Aimee," I said, putting my hands out, "let me explain."

Her eyebrows came together. "How did you get in here? Why do you have a key?"

"It's Isa," I said. "It's your roommate."

She looked at me like she'd seen a very rare and very extinct creature, and then anger clouded her blue eyes. "Seriously? You burned time to look like Katrina Darling?"

I slumped onto my desk chair. "Please don't judge me right now. I can't handle it. Not after the past twenty-four hours."

She angled herself toward me, the comforter pulling around her. "What happened to your arm?"

I glanced down to where the ribbon of my sleeve revealed the angry cut from the claw. "An old Brazilian woman slashed me with a foot-long claw in the coffee shop."

One of the things I liked best about Aimee: she had a strong nurturing instinct. As soon as I'd said it, instead of questioning me further, she leapt from the bed and went straight for the first-aid kit. "Take your shirt off."

"Don't you want to know why an old Brazilian woman attacked me at the coffee shop?" I said from behind the veil of my shirt as I pulled it over my head.

"She's the same woman who came into our English class." Aimee ripped the wrapping off a sanitizing wipe and pressed it to the cut on my arm.

I hissed through my teeth, keeping my eyes on her face instead of what she was doing to my cut; I was a geneticist who hated the sight of blood or the body's insides. Go me. "How'd you know?"

Aimee kept dabbing, intent on the cut. "How many old South American women are wandering around McGill's campus in the middle of winter?"

"Point taken." I watched her with heart-swelling fondness. "I'm glad you're OK after, you know …"

Her blue eyes met mine. "After a giant wolf crashed through the dining hall window?"

I made a face, nodded. "Yeah, that."

She pulled out some sticky white sutures from the kit, pressed them one at a time over my cut. "I don't know what's going on, Isa, but I assume it's an encantado thing. And to be honest, it terrifies me."

My eyebrows went up. She seemed so together at this moment, but now that she'd said it, I saw the slight tremor in her hands. I knew she dealt with strong anxiety all the time; Aimee was just trying to hold it together.

I set my hand on her shoulder. "I think it's best if you sleep elsewhere for the next few nights."

She finished treating my wound, leaned back. "You're kicking me out of our dorm?"

"With the best of intentions."

"That creature was here for you," she said. "I saw it chase you out of the dining hall."

I swallowed. "I think you're right."

"And it'll come back."

"I think it will."

She scrutinized me, her eyes traveling over my face and body. "And why the hell do you look like Katrina Darling?"

"It's a long story." I stood to grab a sweater from my closet—and to put some distance between me and Aimee.

Aimee stood. "You're pretending to be her because she's been gone for the last three weeks." It wasn't a question.

I stood in front of my open closet, staring at the selection of subpar clothing. Nothing in here was anything like what I'd seen Katrina wearing, which was what always seemed to happen when I admired people. I could recreate every detail—the appearance, the wardrobe, the same perfume—but it all felt off-brand on me, like knockoffs. All the magic would go, and it would just be a purse, a sweater, a pair of boots.

"I just wanted to see what it would be like. Just for one night," I said into the void of my closet.

"What did you say?" Aimee said.

I grabbed a sweater, turned back toward her. "I just wanted to see."

She nodded slowly, non-judgmentally. But I could tell that wasn't true, just because I knew Aimee—she didn't approve of what I'd done. "You need to shift back."

"I can't right now." A million reasons flitted through my mind as to why: I had just burned more of my life in that stupid coffee shop to resume my illusion and I wasn't about to give it up this fast; I needed to talk to Justin about what had happened and I had promised to meet him after class. On and on they went, but what they really boiled down to was one thing.

I just didn't want to.

"Why not?" Aimee asked.

I yanked the sweater on, my head popping through the neckhole like a creature being birthed. "Aimee, a woman slashed me with a claw the size of a stalagmite. There's a massive wolf roaming around campus, probably looking for me. Can we focus on those things right now?"

"Do you think they're related?"

I stopped, the sweater half-adorned. "What do you mean?"

"Do you think the old Brazilian woman with the claw has something to do with the wolf?"

I slow-blinked. Then, "Four claws."

"Four claws?" she repeated.

"I think the wolf was missing a claw on its left forepaw."

"Between the growling and the big teeth, I don't recall."

I waved my hands through the air. "Hold on! Let me think." I screwed my eyes shut, recreating the scene in my mind. The creature bursting through the glass, stalking through the dining hall. Chasing us into the street, running above us on the buildings.

There. It was in that moment when I'd glanced up, seen the lobisomem above Justin and me, that I caught a proper view of the left forepaw. It was missing the second claw—the equivalent of its pointer finger being shorn off at the first knuckle.

I opened my eyes, and Aimee and I stared at each other. "Holy shit," I said.

"You're cursing in English. That's never good."

I pulled the sweater fully on. "Well, it isn't good."

This old woman, whoever she was, had received incredible power from her curse. She had somehow ripped the claw from that wolf and attacked me with it.

I was her target. Consequently, I was this creature's target. This creature, whose claws—and probably teeth—could interfere with my illusions. My magic.

I grabbed my coat and bag. "Aimee, promise me you'll find somewhere else to sleep for the next few nights. I don't want it coming here for me and finding you."

She stood from the bed, enfolded me in a hug. "Where are you going?"

I sighed into her arms. "Elsewhere. It's best for you right now if I just stay away."

She leaned back, stared at me. "What do you mean, 'elsewhere?' "

Frankly, I didn't know. I only knew I needed to talk to Justin, to warn him. And a small part of my brain returned: *Do you really need to warn him? Can't you just stay away from him?*

But, like any creature of obsession, the chemically-influenced part of my mind insisted on it. I needed to see him before night came.

I refocused on Aimee. "I'm going to take care of all this."

"Isa, you're not Katrina Darling." Her hands slid to enfold my own. "You're different, and that's OK. You don't have to try to be tough like her."

I squeezed her hands. "Don't worry," I said, which seemed to reassure her. "Just start packing a bag and be out before tonight, OK?"

She nodded. "I'll go to Elisa's."

Our pixie friend Elisa, a sophomore who lived in another dorm. Perfect.

As I stepped out of the dorm, I knew Aimee was right: I wasn't Katrina Darling, and I wouldn't try to be. I would find Justin, deliver my cryptic warning, and get the hell away from the people I cared about.

But first, I had to confirm my suspicions.

CHAPTER SIX

By the time I arrived at the biology building and found Professor Allman's class, it was in full swing. Through the small window, I saw him lifting the furry replica of a hawk.

After a year in his classes, if I knew one thing about that man, it was that he really loved birds—real and imagined.

I stood outside the door, glanced at the wall clock. When had it gotten to be after three? That gave me about two, maybe three hours until dusk. I needed to be well away from Montreal before dusk. At this rate, I wouldn't even make it to the outskirts of the city.

After twenty minutes someone pushed the door open, and out bustled thirty students. I waited until they'd all filed past, and then I stepped into the almost empty biology classroom.

Inside, I found Professor Allman staring back at me, paused in the middle of erasing a whiteboard. He was an older man, two tufts of white hair floating around his head, but his green eyes were sharp, and he had the voice of a much younger man.

"Hello," he said. He should have recognized me, but with a start, I realized I wasn't the Isabella Ramirez he knew. He didn't know me at all. "How can I help you?"

The anxiety of being a stranger to him gripped me in its vise. "I ...

was thinking of signing up for your Other studies biology class, and I had a few questions."

"By all means." He waved me over. "What's your name?"

I came forward, paused before answering. "Katrina Darling."

"Well, Katrina Darling, ask away."

I stepped closer—so close he seemed a little uncomfortable—and leaned toward him across his podium. "Do you know about creatures of South American lore?"

I knew he did; I had been an undergraduate genetics researcher under Professor Allman for the past year and a half, and that continent was the man's obsession. The quickest way to derail one of his train of thought was to start asking about the curupira, a small, redheaded creature of the forests of Brazil with backward feet. It liked to confuse hunters by making tracks in the wrong direction. It also had a hell of a whistle.

Even though he knew I was an Other, Professor Allman didn't believe the curupira existed. Someday, I thought as his eyes lit up, I should tell him that I'd known a whole family of them.

"Sounds like you've heard about my first love, " he said. "What do you want to know?"

"Have you heard of the lobisomem?"

He nodded at once. "A werewolf of Brazilian legend. Apparently a very unpleasant looking monkey in its human form."

"A were-monkey?"

"No, a werewolf. But yes, its other form is a monkey, and since we generally assume that werewolves are human-to-wolf and vice versa, I see the confusion." Then he murmured to himself, "I really should try to coin a phrase—something like Monkwolf. It could become a thing. It may even ... what do you kids call it?" He snapped his fingers. "Go viral."

I had no idea what *we kids* called anything. If this older human was out of touch, what did it make my five-hundred-year-old self? Out of everything. This, despite my roommate's frantic efforts to sit me in front of as many popular movies as she could. "Your education in humanity," Aimee called it. Though I felt doubtful about *Jurassic Park* helping me to understand humans better.

"Werewolf," I repeated. "So the lobisomem only changes by the light of the full moon?"

"Some do," he said. "It depends on the creature, and most especially on whether it's cursed."

"What about one that can appear during the day? And has claws that can nullify magic?"

His green eyes went wide with delight. "You're referring to El Lobizon."

I swallowed. "El Lobizon," I repeated. Any creature of lore with an article preceding its name—in this case, *el*—meant unique power.

"A terrible, cursed creature," he went on. "You see, El Lobizon is always under the control of the master who summoned it. In that way, it can assume its deadliest form at any time of the night—or the day. And that's not the worst part."

I waited, but he only gathered up his bag and started toward the door.

"Where are you going?" I asked. "What's the worst part?"

"Come with me, Katrina," he said. "I have a book in my office that you'll love."

Love, I thought, *is one way of putting it.*

↔

We took two flights of stairs, my hands shaking as we walked, and not because of the cold—well, not just because of the cold; I am Brazilian, after all.

It was because I had just burned two months of my life and, in the process, had provided a scent trail for a creature who I suspected could completely dismantle my illusions. My way of life.

Professor Allman led us into a small, single-window cranny of an office on the fourth floor. Little did he know, I'd been here many times; this was where we had weekly meetings to discuss my ongoing research on Other DNA. Here, of all places, was where I felt safest. Where I could spend hours being myself without fear of judgment or the gig being up.

That was kind of an Other thing in this GoneGod World: we were often afraid of the gig being up, the other shoe dropping, the humans around us turning murderous. It had happened quite a lot around the world since the GrandExodus—and with more frequency in recent years.

So it was saying a lot that Aimee was my best friend.

When I stepped inside, billowing warmth and the familiar scent of books washed over me. It was also profoundly quiet, which, as an introvert, I'd always found centering, comforting.

Maybe that was why I still opted for real books. Or maybe it was because I still preferred the 19th century (well, except for the whole modern medicine thing). Whichever it was, I calmed a little as Professor Allman turned on the light and gestured for me to sit in the overstuffed armchair.

"Let me see." He ran his finger over the spines of a dozen different books on one of the shelves as I dropped into the seat, rubbing at my amulet.

After a minute, he let an "Ah," plucked a small book from the shelf and set it in my lap. "Turn to page fifty-eight."

I glanced at the cover: *Creatures of Amazonian Lore.* I flipped the pages, the pictures sailing by until I stabbed a finger between two leaves. I lifted my finger as the book settled on its spine, and a wolf with red eyes stared back. Cold recognition ran through me, and my eyes flicked to the name.

El Lobizon, the hunter.

"Is that what you were thinking of?" he asked cheerfully.

"Yes," I whispered, reading as fast as my eyes could process.

El Lobizon had to be summoned, and remained fully under the power and direction of his master. His greatest power—one even the

RAMY VANCE

angels feared—was his ability to nullify magic. His presence alone had that effect, though it wasn't clear how large his radius was.

Thinking back, I had felt his effects from the other side of the dining hall. That had been at least twenty feet. Maybe Justin hadn't noticed anything because of the lack of light under the table, or because a killer wolf was stalking through the building, but my illusion had definitely been affected.

I lifted my pocket mirror out of my purse, opened it to observe myself. Still Katrina Darling, right down to the freckle below her left eye. So even though I'd taken a direct wound, the magical nullification hadn't persisted.

But as I read on, a point of greater concern leapt from the page: El Lobizon's canines. With one bite, his venom would strip the prey of all magical abilities. Not just for hours or days, but forever.

That was what the angels feared. That was what I had narrowly escaped.

While he could hunt during the day, El Lobizon became most powerful after sundown, his night vision so potent he became a fearsome hunter. Night was when he came into his own.

And the worst thing of all: he could discern one magical scent from another—all bore a stamp as unique as a human fingerprint—and once he caught wind of his prey's scent, he didn't stop. Not until El Lobizon caught his quarry or his summoner freed him from his bondage.

My first thought was of Justin. We had spent the night together, our bodies enfolded about as closely as two people could be. My scent was all over him.

And Aimee. She had touched me when she was treating my wound and hugged me after.

My eyes flicked to the square window on my left, where outside the day had slipped into late afternoon. Pale light issued through the panes, and it would soon grow paler.

Someone—likely that elderly woman—had summoned El Lobizon here in Montreal, and it knew my scent with unmistakable acuteness. After all, I had just burned two months of my life to become Katrina

46

Darling. That was the equivalent of placing a 24-hour cookie shop at the center of a college campus.

I swallowed. I had all the trappings of Katrina, but none of her monster-fighting prowess. So I did the thing I was best at. (Well, one of them.)

I leapt from the chair. "Professor, can I hold on to this book for a little while?"

"Why, sure. If you'll just bring it back to my—"

"To your office. Got it," I said, weaving past him. If I survived all this, I would eventually have to explain to Allman and all my other professors what was going on. Why Isabella Ramirez had disappeared from their classes for a few days, and why Katrina Darling was borrowing a book that Isabella would eventually return.

If I survived all this.

I hurried back to my dorm and took the most unpleasantly scalding shower of my life. Fortunately, Aimee had vacated as I'd told her to—I couldn't handle her questioning me right now, not to mention the danger it would put her in—and I made liberal use of her loofah to scrub myself from scalp to toes. By the time I got out, I looked pinker than some of my encantado sisters in their natural forms.

In the shower, I had used Aimee's shampoo, and afterward, covered myself in her body lotion. If El Lobizon was after me—and Aimee, by extension—then I would be both her and me.

I would be Aimee's scent squared.

That was why, before I headed to the O³ house, I opened her dresser drawer, grabbed a pair of her jeans, a sweater and the extra coat she'd hung on the door. It was why I grabbed up her perfume bottle and sprayed myself in its mist until I smelled like a fake floral arrangement.

Like I said, this was what I did best: pretend to be someone else.

CHAPTER SEVEN

*T*he massive lion's head door knocker clomped against the wood once, twice, three times. I cringed every time, glancing over one shoulder and then the other; the thing sounded like a struck gong.

Ten seconds later, a built blond guy opened the door and looked down at me. His nose wrinkled as the perfume-o-rama swirling around me hit his nostrils, but to his credit, he only said, "Hey. Kat, right?"

"Right. Is Justin here?"

He gestured me into a frat house out of the movies. The two-storied foyer included a wide, winding mahogany staircase. The walls had been adorned with O^3 banners, each of them signifying a different class. Someone had set a pair of crossed paddles on the wall, and if I were a betting gal (which I was), I'd say they had been used for smacking.

Which was a bizarrely erotic college convention. Not that these frat guys would ever admit as much.

"Hey, Justin!" The blond called up the stairs. "Your girl's here."

I stood below, gripping my purse until Justin's face appeared at the top of the stairs. He set both hands on the rail, and when his eyes found me, the look of concern and relief that swept over his brow made my heart skip.

"Hey," I called up to him. He'd already started down the stairs toward me. "Can I come up?"

The blond cupped his hands to his mouth, let out an *oooh* that reddened my face. I flashed a look at him over my shoulder—my best sultry encantado glance—and he dropped his hands, cleared his throat.

"What was that, boy-o?" I said.

He could barely meet my eyes, and I knew I'd had *that* effect on him. He couldn't stop smiling. "Just that you're always welcome at the O³ house, Kat. I'm sure Justin agrees." He fought a grin.

"Yeah, come up," Justin said. He'd reached the bottom of the stairs on double-time, grabbed my hand.

I yanked my hand away. "Don't." I felt bad at once, but I couldn't risk him getting my scent on him again. And I also couldn't explain to blondie why that was. "It's a long story," I whispered.

Justin looked hurt, but like any good athlete, he shrugged it off and nodded me toward the staircase. "You can tell me all about it."

I followed him to the second floor, watching the dictionary definition of a V-shaped back ascend the stairs ahead of me. I blinked hard, trying to keep my mind on the issues at hand: El Lobizon, and the very real possibility that Justin would soon find out I wasn't Katrina Darling.

Justin led me into his bedroom, which I properly observed for the first time. It was surprisingly neat and austere for a frat house guy's place: a queen-sized bed with a navy comforter as the room's centerpiece, two windows flanking the headboard, a dresser and a lamp.

On his bedside table, a framed picture of him and Kat. It looked like she'd been taking a selfie of the two of them, and he had surprised her with a kiss. The whole thing—the print, the frame—was very retro and wholesome.

Which was why it killed me that I'd instituted a no-touching rule. All I wanted to do was throw myself at Justin Truly, to repeat last night.

"Come sit." He dropped onto the end of his bed and patted the spot beside him.

"I shouldn't." I stood in the same pose I'd been in in the foyer, both hands on the strap of my purse.

He sighed, leaned forward with his elbows on his knees. "OK Kat, what's up with you? I mean, aside from the fact that we were chased by a wolf the size of a mountain, and then you spent an hour in the bathroom after you knocked our coffee over and then yelled at me in Spanish."

"It was Portuguese."

"You know Portuguese?"

Merda. The lies just kept piling up. "I've studied it some."

"OK—Portuguese, then. What happened there, anyway? You just leapt up and ran off, and the noises coming from the bathroom ..."

I pulled up the sleeve of my sweater—which was much easier to do now that I was Katrina-sized—until the wound on my arm was exposed to the light. "She did this to me."

He half-stood, but I stepped back. So he just stared at my scratch from where he was. "Who did? How?"

"You couldn't see her—which is a long story—but there was a woman with a massive claw. The claw of that giant wolf we were attacked by yesterday in the dining hall."

"The lobi ..."

"Not just the lobisomem—El Lobizon," I said. "I believe she's controlling it. And I need to deal with this situation tonight. Justin, I need you to do something right away."

I had just thrown a ton of information at him, and he looked dizzy. But an admirable second later, one black eyebrow rose, and he waited for me to continue.

"I need you to strip off all your clothes and scrub yourself from head to toe in the shower."

He let a bark of a laugh. "Is this some sort of foreplay?"

I wished. "No," I said. "This is something I need you to do to protect yourself. The thing is, that wolf has my scent. It's after me, and you have my scent on you."

It wasn't the whole truth—I had left out the part about my *magical* scent—but some part of me still felt unwilling to tell him everything. I had burned two months of my life to be Katrina Darling, after all.

I wanted him to believe I was this brave. That I would confront the creature.

"How can I still have your scent on me?" he said. "I showered this morning."

"We touched after your shower, too, and it can smell that. Imagine a regular wolf's scenting capabilities, and then square that. Twice."

He looked confused. "Uh, that makes…"

"It means anyone I've touched since he was summoned, he can smell the residue of that touch. And he won't stop until he gets his prey—and any other creature that smells like his prey."

"Well then." He stood. When he pulled off his shirt and the swath of his chest came into view, I had to set a hand on the dresser. I quickly snatched it away; I'd just introduced more of my scent in his room. "How did you become that thing's prey, Kat?"

"It's a really, really long story," I said. "And I can't stay right now to tell you the whole thing."

He unbuckled his belt, and I tried desperately to keep my eyes on his face. I failed. "Where are you going? Does it have something to do with where you've been?"

I'm going to run away, I thought. *I'm going to hide, to evade, do like I always do: slip into the shadows until the problem goes away.*

But I was pretending to be Katrina Darling, so I said, "I can't tell you where I'm going, but I can say I'm going to fight it."

He stepped toward me, and I stepped back with clenched teeth. "What's your plan?"

"I'm going to find El Lobizon's summoner, and I'm going to defeat her. Preferably with words. Maybe baked goods."

I could tell he wanted to be amused, but he was too worried. Which was quite a contrast with his actions, which were to take off his pants, and then …

Que bonito! I turned away, shielding my eyes.

51

"Nothing you haven't seen before, babe," he murmured. "Talk to me while I'm in the shower, OK?"

Oh, that was going to be so much easier than talking to a slowly-stripping-to-nude Justin. But I dutifully stood in the doorway while he showered, the only things blocking his bits from me a plastic curtain with blue squares and a whole lot of steam.

"Kat, take me with you," he said over the water. "I know last time turned out terribly, but I don't want you to do this alone."

Last time? I wondered what he meant by that, and I thought back to how he had listened to me when I'd asked him to leave me alone in the bathroom of the cafe. I'd only gotten glimpses of what had happened between him and Kat—not enough to do much more than speculate. And I didn't have time to ask him right now; I just needed to disappear for a few days until I got this whole situation under control.

"I'm sorry, Justin," I said, "but I can't bring you along. I need you to go to your parents' house for the weekend."

He turned toward me in the middle of scrubbing his hair, white foam dripping onto his face. "Leave Montreal? Seriously?"

Good—his parents weren't in the city. "Because El Lobizon might come after you in an effort to get to me." And because I wouldn't be in Montreal myself. I would be gone, gone, gone, and when I reappeared —whenever that would be—I would have found a way to slip the noose.

"Don't be ridiculous. I'm not letting you go after that creature alone."

I sighed. "I'm Cherub, remember? It'll take more than an oversized dog to put me down."

Oh, how I wished I were actually Cherub.

"I know you're tough. A lot tougher than me," he said, still rubbing at his scalp, "but it seems so wrong to let you do this by yourself. What about Deirdre? Egya?"

Deirdre. That was Kat's roommate, who I also hadn't seen in weeks. And I had no idea who Egya was.

"I don't want to endanger anyone else," I said. "Just make sure you pack a bag and head to your parents' tonight, OK?"

He plucked a triangle of curtain aside to stare at me. "You're sure you can deal with this?"

I nodded. "I'm sure."

"OK." He closed the curtain and turned toward the shower head, dousing his face in its spray. "But don't go before I get a chance to say a proper goodbye. I won't touch you—I just want to be out of the shower before you leave."

Justin, I thought, *why do you do this to me?*

"I won't go," I promised.

But that was exactly what I did. I disappeared amidst the sounds of the water and Justin scrubbing himself clean of my magical scent.

Wouldn't be the first time a man has done that, I thought on my way down the stairs. But of course, the first time a man had scrubbed himself clean of my scent had been for different reasons entirely.

CHAPTER EIGHT

$\mathcal{I}$ shielded my eyes from the setting sun as I stepped into Montreal's terminal. The next bus out of the city would depart in a half-hour, which meant I'd be traveling at 60 mph away from all this.

That was probably faster than El Lobizon could run. Probably.

I purchased my ticket to Quebec City, took a seat on one of the empty benches with my purse set in my lap. I hadn't brought anything except my wallet, my phone, Professor Allman's book on creatures of Amazonian lore and a single change of clothes.

I had disappeared with less before.

The sky shone pink and yellow through the tall windows of the terminal, and I was shivering again. At any moment I expected the glass to cave inward, El Lobizon's giant form to come barreling into the center of the terminal and for it to sink its incisors right through my head.

And every moment that it didn't happen, I felt a little tighter strung, like a drum so taut it would barely produce any vibration at all.

I pulled Professor Allman's book out of my bag, continued reading the entry on El Lobizon. To defeat the creature, it read, the prey must find and confront El Lobizon's summoner.

Just as I suspected. It was as simple as that: confrontation. Which also happened to be my worst skill.

"Anyone sitting here?" came a soft voice.

I jumped, pulled the book to my chest. When I looked up, an old woman's face stared back down at me. White-haired, lined cheeks, a close-lipped—sincere—smile on her face. A bulging bag hung off her shoulder.

Not the Brazilian woman. Just an old woman.

She was homeless. And she had deep crow's feet at the corners of both eyes. *Harmless,* I thought at once.

I glanced at the long swath of empty bench. "Please." I gestured left of me.

She deposited her bags, sat closer than most people would have. Except she didn't press me for money or conversation. She just wanted to be seen, I realized. Just to be seen.

I lowered the book back to my lap, where the dark portrait of El Lobizon stared back up at me. And then I diverted my eyes to the woman beside me. "Where are you going?" I asked her.

"Nowhere. Just here," she said, her hands now folded in her lap. She was staring out the windows ahead of us. "Where are you going?"

"Quebec City."

"Visiting a boyfriend?"

"Leaving one, actually."

"Oh." She nodded. Something about her voice came clear and lucid and calming, which I hadn't expected. "I did that a few times."

"It's not like that," I said quickly. "I care about him."

"But you're leaving."

"I have to leave."

Her eyes shifted to me. "Why do you have to leave someone you care about?"

"It's hard to explain."

"Is he good to you?"

"Yes. But there are a few reasons I have to go."

She let a small exhale of amusement. "There always are, aren't there?"

"What do you mean?"

She turned toward me in full. "How old are you?"

"I, well …" How to explain my age? I had been alive for over five hundred years, though only a few as a mortal. "I'm twenty-one," I said finally. That was sort of true, since the gods had only left a few years ago, and I had usually taken the illusion of eighteen- to twenty-one-year-old women.

"I was twenty years older than you when I realized I was the constant."

I stared. "The constant?"

"I kept leaving people behind, and I always thought I had good reasons." She pointed at herself, and her eyebrows went up. "But eventually I ended up alone, and I was the constant in every situation. Do you see what I mean?"

I slow-blinked. "No."

"Once you have enough history behind you, you will."

"Is this like that saying, 'if everyone around you is an asshole, then you're the asshole?'"

She laughed a little. "I guess it is."

I sat back against the bench, staring through the windows. The sun had dropped fully out of view, and shades of blue were slowly sapping the color out of the sky.

In my purse, my phone vibrated once. A text message. I lifted it out, found two lines from Aimee: *elisa's not around and I don't have a key. I can't afford a hostel, so I'm going to sleep in the lab like that one time. I'll be sure to lock it behind me … That should be OK, right?*

No, I thought. *No, no, no.* Walking between Elisa's and the lab where I did my research would take Aimee through Old Montreal, by the river.

that's not far enough, I texted back. *where are you?*

walking back from her place. will be there soon, came the reply a minute later.

She was already outside, walking through the campus in the dark. I mentally traced the route from Elisa's to the lab; as I'd thought, the walk would take her right along the river.

56

get to the nearest underground entrance, I texted, *and stay down there until I find you.*

I threw my phone and the book in my purse, looked over at the woman beside me. "I'm the asshole," I said as I stood.

She watched me stand. "What?"

I grabbed my wallet, pulled out all the cash I had—about fifty dollars—and handed it to her. "I'm the asshole," I repeated. "Please, find some place to sleep tonight."

She stared at the money, then at me. "Do you think I'm homeless?"

I half-lowered my hand. "Uh, well, I … "

She let a bark of a laugh. "Oh, dear. You're very sweet, but I have a home. I just like to people-watch."

Tinder sparked in my chest. "So even though you were the asshole, you didn't end up alone."

"No," she said. "I had to work very hard at changing, though."

I nodded. "I'm going to try to do that tonight."

"You're going to stick around?"

"I'm going to confront the woman who summoned El Lobizon, and I'm going to protect my friend from being attacked or killed by his deadly claws and canines."

She nodded, and her eyes took on a particular glaze. "That's good, dear. Be safe walking outside in the dark."

She thought I was drunk or high. Maybe both.

I smiled down at her. Before I turned and darted through the terminal doors, I set my hand over hers. "I'll do my best."

↔

I set out into the night, my phone clutched tight in my hand, waiting for Aimee's text.

My breath came in white puffs, and tiny flakes of snow began to fall on the already frozen earth. Above me, the sky had turned to the deep azure preceding nightfall.

I walked fast through the campus toward the biology building. If I took the right route, I might be able to intercept Aimee on her—

A howl pierced the night like a knife. I froze in place. Around me, nothing had changed: people walked huddled on the sidewalks, cars left slushy tracks in the street, and the moon cast its yellow glow over the city.

The moon. My eyes lifted to it on the horizon, where it sat as round as an orange, and I wondered if it was all just coincidence.

Becoming Katrina Darling. El Lobizon. The Brazilian woman who wanted me dead. All of it converging on this night, when the moon happened to be as round as an eyeball.

The howl had come from the east—the direction of the river. That was where I needed to go, but I remained stuck in place. If I went that way, I sensed everything would happen quickly. And I might not survive the night.

After all, I wasn't Katrina Darling.

I wasn't a fighter. I was a runner.

My phone buzzed, and I lifted it to find a text from Justin. *everything ok?*

I stood on the sidewalk, yanking off my glove to write back. *yes. did you leave town?*

Almost instantly, the reassuring triple dots popped up. *I couldn't. kat, I heard the howl. tell me where you are*

what?? just go! I wrote back.

if you don't tell me where you are, I'm going to drive in the direction i heard it with your hat on my head and the windows down

I had forgotten my hat? My hand went to my head, where I found only Aimee's earmuffs. I had put on my own beanie when I left the dorm, and then left it sitting in Justin's bedroom like a doofus.

you wouldnt, I wrote. *it's dangerous, justin*

i love you, kat. i couldn't just leave you here alone, knowing what you're facing

He loved me? He loved me. Well, he loved Katrina, but the words struck me with the same resonance as if he had written my own name. Because right now, I was Kat.

i'm walking to Old Montreal, I wrote. *Aimee is by the river.*

A few seconds later, a one-word reply: *coming.*

He was coming. The knowledge terrified me as much as it warmed me. Now, the two people I cared about most were in the exact place I didn't want them to be.

I pulled my glove back on and started into a jog down the street, staring at every face I passed in the hope that it would be Aimee's. But none were her, and it wasn't until I neared the river that I heard a scream.

Her scream.

Followed by a snarl.

I came around the bend, and the scene before me couldn't have been more nightmarish.

The Brazilian woman, her white hair floating around her like it had caught a breeze. (There was no breeze.) She faced down Aimee, who stood twenty feet away, both hands up as if she was being mugged. (She wasn't being mugged.)

It was worse than being mugged.

Between them stood El Lobizon, head lowered, hackles up. He stalked toward her with the slow assurance of a predator whose prey was already caught.

None of them had seen me, and none would unless I announced myself. I could watch the whole scene like a play and then slip back the way I had come.

Then, an irritating thought: *What would Katrina Darling do?*

Where had that come from? Was I becoming religious in my mortality? Why was Katrina Darling whose actions I wanted to emulate?

Then, the response: *Because you admire her.*

Not just the way she dressed or her hair or her boyfriend. I admired her bravery, her guts, even her GoneGodDamn quips at the worst moments in English class.

I surveyed Aimee, the woman, the wolf, the frozen river running beside them, and after a time, a wild, unlikely thought came to me.

Katrina Darling would come up with a plan.

I stepped up to the sidewalk, lifted a mittened hand and pointed at El Lobizon. "Hey, you son of a bitch! (That would offend a dog, too, right?) Get away from my friend."

That should have done it.

El Lobizon spun, his black pupils locking onto me. The Brazilian woman turned. Aimee's eyes lighted on me.

And then, the last thing I wanted to hear: the old woman let a careening laugh. It was the kind of noise a person with nothing to lose might make, and I realized I was in way, way over my head.

CHAPTER NINE

"*Ela é sua presa!*" the old woman shouted, her bare hand rising toward me, one finger emerging from the folds of her dress to point at the center of my chest.

El Lobizon half-lowered before he sprang toward me, his claws raking divots in the sidewalk as he began his hunt.

So I did what any encantado would do.

I let out a shriek and turned, running down the sidewalk as fast as my heeled boots would take me. I'm sure, with my hands swinging and my slip-sliding on the ice, I looked ridiculous.

And later, when Aimee asked me about it, I would say I meant to look ridiculous. But I hadn't—I was actually running for my life in the best (most absurd) way I knew how when running down an icy sidewalk.

But I did have a plan.

I only needed to take El Lobizon far enough from Aimee that she wouldn't get hurt. But I wasn't sure if I could run very far before he caught up to me.

I glanced over my shoulder; El Lobizon wasn't fifty feet away, and he would close the space between us in just a few seconds.

I stopped hard beside the river, turning toward it. As I did, floodlights illuminated behind me, sending the frozen river and the far bank into relief. What the hell was that? But I didn't have time to consider it; I would be dead in a moment.

I ran down the side of the bank and squeezed my eyes shut as I leapt in. Magic poured out of me, sliding over my body in a warm, enfolding wave. When my feet hit the ice, they sank right through and I slipped into the fantastically cold water beneath.

I opened my eyes for an excruciating second beneath the water— just as a massive form crashed through the ice beside me. El Lobizon, plowing into the canal like a missile.

A moment later, my body had reverted to its truest form. It's natural form. The encantado form.

I was in my element.

↔

GoneGodDamn was it cold. But I could handle it for about a minute, which was long enough.

Even as a creature of the Brazilian rainforest, the encantado's natural form was highly resistant to heat or cold. Like dolphins, our lower bodies had an extra layer of adipose tissue and a slick skin that would encase it.

Which El Lobizon didn't have. His great, black coat of fur absorbed the cold water like a paper towel as he clawed ineffectually under the surface, those red eyes glaring like they could burn holes in me.

But he couldn't draw himself any closer to me, where with a little flip of my tail, I could have easily maneuvered myself well out of his reach.

"Hunt this!" I said—except in my encantado form, it was really more like a series of dolphin squeaks —and angled my tail to thrust a strong current of water toward him.

A second later, the current pushed him back, and I saw the bubbles rise from his mouth as he growled. Already his pawing had slowed as his fur dragged him down, the cold seeping into his massive muscles.

Another minute and he would freeze under here, and that would be the end of El Lobizon.

I had just begun swimming toward the hole in the ice when a second, smaller form burst through next to the creature.

A human. Black-haired, tall and muscular.

Justin Truly, that idiot, had jumped into the freezing canal to save me.

↔

As soon as he'd entered the water, I could tell Justin regretted his choice. He took one brave look around before he spotted El Lobizon, and then me. I saw him blink once, and he began an air-breathing mammal's familiar, desperate scramble toward the surface.

But he wouldn't make it; he was wearing jeans and a sweater. And Justin had jumped in right next to the creature, who was still trying to get to me—his prey. The creature paddled like a dog, one terrific paw knocking Justin in the process, who sailed toward the darkness at the bottom of the river.

"No!" I screamed, and with a single flip of my tail, I pelted through the water toward him.

The cold was already affecting my ability to swim, but I burned magic as I raced toward Justin, and the familiar warmth of it sailing over my body gave me just enough energy to veer past El Lobizon and reach Justin.

I took hold of his sweater in my rapidly freezing arms and, with the most exhausting tail-flip of my long life, brought us both toward the massive hole El Lobizon had created when he'd leapt into the river.

We surfaced together, and I had just enough energy to get us halfway onto the icy surface. Justin had fallen unconscious—whether from the blow from the creature's paw or from shock, I couldn't tell.

I gasped as the night air touched my human half. I didn't have long before I would freeze to death. I kept hold of Justin's sweater, trying to pull the two of us out onto the surface, but I didn't have the strength.

I gave a final flick of my tail, but I was too weak—I had exhausted everything.

"Encantado!" came a familiar voice. Ahead of me, the old woman had picked her way to the edge of the water, and was sliding across the ice toward us. I didn't know what her intentions were, but none of that mattered to me right now.

I only wanted to get out of the water. Needed to get out.

She dropped to her knees, crawl-sliding toward my outreached, shaking arm.

When her hand grabbed mine, I hardly felt it. My other arm was still around Justin, and she pulled us the rest of the way out of the water and onto the ice with amazing strength.

I lay there on my back, unable and unwilling to move anything except my eyes. Above us, the night sky, and in my periphery, the old Brazilian woman knelt beside us. Staring at me.

Why? Why did she want me dead so badly?

"Watch out," I tried to say to Justin, but it came out as a faint exhale. I was going into shock, I realized, as the moon and stars faded in my vision.

The last thing I heard before the darkness took me were the faint sounds of knocking. El Lobizon under the ice, still struggling, still seeking his prey.

CHAPTER TEN

I woke to a woman's soft humming, a candle's light and warmth. It issued around me like a blanket, and I realized I was feeling heat from a vent.

Ah, modern living was a remarkable thing. Humans sometimes voiced a little fondness for it, but they couldn't appreciate it like a once-immortal Other could.

Wait, where was I? The memories returned to me with a start: El Lobizon, the river, rescuing Justin from the water, the old woman sliding across the ice. And at the end, her face over me, blocking the moon.

My hand went to the amulet at my neck, found it still there. I rubbed it as my eyes traveled around the space. I was in a kitchen. Or, more accurately, on a chair with a blanket wrapped around me. I peeked inside the blanket and discovered Katrina Darling's naked body—my body. At some point in my semi-unconscious (or maybe completely unconscious) delirium, I had shifted back to her. My hair was wet, and when I wiggled my fingers and toes, I found them functional, but I couldn't get up.

Every part of me felt exhausted, just barely above hypothermic. All I wanted to do was sleep.

But that humming continued through the dark doorway, and it kept me awake. Beside me, a square table and four chairs, a row of cabinets, and above, a single fluorescent bulb diffused by a floral glass cover.

The voice neared, and I recognized it as an old village song from Brazil. Centuries old, a favorite among women as they went about the house, cooking or maybe sweeping.

"Hello?" I called.

"Ah, feiticeira," came a voice. *"Enchantress,"* she had called me. A slippered foot stepped into the room. "You're awake."

My gaze flitted from the feet straight up the length of her body, and I squinted my eyes shut when I saw that face.

It was her. White-haired, those dark, haunted eyes. She stared at me with folded-arm triumph.

"Você convocou a criatura," I said.

She offered a single nod. "I summon him," she said in English. Her voice creaked like a book's spine being tested for the first time in decades.

"Why?"

She slipped back into Portuguese. "I hear your kind is marvelous at recognizing faces. Do you remember me, encantado?"

I studied her face. Just as when I'd seen her the first time, something about her eyes struck me as familiar, but I felt certain I hadn't met her before—not in my mortal or immortal life. I had left Brazil back when the gods left, and I hadn't returned since.

"I …"

"You don't. I seem familiar, but in a way you can't place." She shrugged her narrow shoulders. "Then how about this?"

She shuffled forward in that old dress, lowered with great care and effort so our faces were level, and reached out her hands toward my face. "Oh, lover," she crooned. "You're a bird. A gift."

My throat caught. It couldn't be.

"Federico," I breathed. And as I said it, I smelled him. That particular scent, what had drawn me to him from the beginning: cinnamon spice and an earthy musk.

It had been seventy years.

I stared into her eyes—*his* eyes, green and flecked with gold. He wielded that gaze like a soldier his sword, and it only took one walk along the river, us meeting eyes that one time, to hew me through and through.

Federico of the long walks by the water. Federico of the green eyes and blue-black hair.

I had loved him with my entire body. Every fiber, every nerve, my thoughts coagulating into him.

The twinge of a smile caught on her face—his smile—and disappeared as quickly. "There we are. Now you remember."

"You're ..."

"Inez. His daughter."

↔

Daughter, I thought, my eyes on the silver strands of her hair floating under the light. A word that implied youth, vitality. Of course, all humans were someone's daughter, from the start to the end. Even white-haired and near that end.

"I knew it was you." Inez pressed my hair from my eyes. "I knew it was you in that other form, with the red hair. Just as surely as I knew it was you in this one."

She was referring to my old appearance, and now to Katrina Darling's.

"What happened to Feddy?"

"My father? Oh, he's dead. Decades ago of lung cancer, while his hair was still a little black. But you might say he died long before that."

My last memory of Federico: the half-full pack of cigarettes sailing out his shirt pocket as he ran. He had rolled them himself, took great pride in every part of their creation. The rolling, the padding of the tobacco, the licking and of course, the smoking.

"I didn't know he had a family," I whispered.

Her top lip lifted, yellowed teeth baring in a snarl. "You wouldn't, would you? Two daughters, a wife who adored him so completely she died of heartbreak when he disappeared. That was how it happened: one night, just gone from the house. By the time he returned a year later, we were in ruin."

Federico. Always impulsive.

He had told me he burned for me. He would give up his job on the coffee plantation, what put the calluses on his hands, what had brought him back and forth along the river each day. This was after I'd taken on the illusion of the young woman with the auburn hair and the delicate frame.

From the moment he had seen me that way, he'd wanted to wrap himself around me at every moment. Of course, he had only come to the river at night. Always at night, where we walked, talked about leaving the village for a secluded life. Together, the two of us.

No mention of family. Of daughters.

And one night, after months, we had done just that. He had a bag when he arrived at the river, he grabbed my hand, and we'd left together. Left the village and made a life together deep in the Brazilian forest for a year.

1943. That shining, gilded time. The world was at war, but we were in love.

"I didn't know," I said again. Inez was lifting something from the folds of her dress now, and a familiar curved edge came into view. Bone-white, as long as my forearm. "Inez, please. Where's Justin?"

"Justin? Ah, the black-haired boy. You like them black-haired." Inez palmed El Lobizon's claw in both hands. "He was your next victim. Wasn't he, encantado?"

"I just want to know if he's all right."

"You will show him what you are before I drive this through your deceitful heart," she said. "And if you refuse, I will make you show him. You remember the creature's magic."

I shuddered, my eyes on the glinting tip of the claw in the kitchen light. I wanted to run, but as young as I was and as old as she was, I didn't think I could even stand. My body was just too tired.

She rose to her full height, the claw disappearing into the folds of her dress before she vanished through the doorway.

I tried to stand anyway, but my limbs felt like sandbags. I could barely move at all. "Help!" I called, my strangled voice echoing in the small kitchen.

Half a minute later, she returned leading a wet-haired Justin into the room, still dazed and shivering. He held a blanket tight around him.

"Here," Inez said in English. "Your love."

↔

I made to rise from the chair, but Inez stepped forward with a strange affect of concern. "No move. Weak."

Justin came forward, hands out, and mine rose to his. He felt so cold as he slumped into the chair next to me. "Are you okay?" His words were slurred from the shock—and likely hypothermia.

"I'm all right." My eyes flicked past him to Inez, whose hands were folded together before her. I needed to play along. "Where are we?"

"Inez saw us in the river," Justin said. "She and Aimee helped get us here in Inez's car. She doesn't speak much English."

"Where's Aimee?" I asked.

"She return home," Inez said. "I take care."

"But you didn't take care of us." I pulled the blanket tighter around me, surveying the room for weapons. The counters were strangely empty, bare. Still, there were two of us and only one of Inez, which meant she couldn't overpower us. Probably. "You should have called the police. Taken us to the hospital."

"So sorry—I am not familiar," Inez explained. "I am from small village in Brazil."

"It's fine, Inez," Justin said, taking a slow, laborious blink. "We're both OK."

"We need to go home now." I tried to stand from the chair. My muscles were on fire, and needles pricked the bottoms of my bare feet.

Inez stepped forward, the deadly tip of El Lobizon's claw emerging in her hand and all pretense gone. *"Não até você mostrar a ele o que você é."*

"Saia do meu caminho," I shot back. I swallowed, turned to Justin. "Help me up."

"What is she talking about, Kat?" Justin asked, his eyes on me. "And since when do you speak Spanish?"

"It's Portuguese." I grabbed his arm. "Let's go."

"Show!" Inez bellowed in English, lifting the tip of the claw to my cheek. *"Mostre-lhe, enganador,"* she murmured. "Show him."

I froze, afraid to move for fear of the tip piercing me. I couldn't take my eyes off the deadly claw. "You have to understand about your father," I whispered in Portuguese. "Let me tell you the truth."

"You stole him. You destroyed my mother," Inez breathed, her chin dimpling with feeling. Her hand shook. "Do you know what it's like to grow up an orphan, you vile bitch?"

"I loved him."

"You're too afraid to show this one the truth, I see. At least he will know what you are before you die."

The next moment happened quickly: with a single motion, she jerked the claw down the side of my face, and my illusion fell away from me like a chocolate coating. A billow of smoke rose into the kitchen, so much I was surprised the smoke alarm didn't go off.

I slipped into the blanket, slid onto the floor. From above, I saw Justin's wide eyes on me as I became the very creature that had driven Federico away seventy years ago.

"Vile bitch," Inez's voice rang through my mind. And then Federico's voice, still so clear after all those decades: "A monster!"

Monster.

In 1943, and in the hundreds of years I lived before the gods' departure, there weren't Others and monsters. The two were one and the same, and in South America, the encantado was as feared as she was repulsive.

Without thinking, I opened my mouth to call out to Justin, but I had already lost my voice. All that came out were a series of incomprehensible squeaks, and the two humans clapped their hands to their ears.

Justin's eyes had gone wide as coins. And Inez dropped to her knees, the claw clasped in both hands and raising high, higher, as high as her arms could go so that when she plunged it into me, the claw would become a dagger. An instrument of death.

If I were Katrina Darling, I would find a way out. To survive. Or at the very least, I'd face this with defiance.

But I wasn't her, and I never would be. So I did the only thing I had left to me to do.

I closed my eyes against the violence, the promise of impossible pain and a quick death. And where, every night in seventy years I'd seen Federico's face, for once I did not.

I saw someone else's face. *As a last look,* I thought, *this isn't a bad way to go.*

CHAPTER ELEVEN

$\mathscr{I}$ didn't die.

A thud sounded on the kitchen tile, followed by a chilling scream from Inez. When I opened my eyes, she and Justin were struggling on the floor in the strangest, half-obscene thing I'd ever seen.

He'd lost or thrown off his blanket, and his naked body gleamed under the light as he tried to pin Inez down, El Lobizon's claw still clutched in her hand. She yelled, "Stop! *Eu esperei tanto tempo.* Stop—stop!"

But of course Justin didn't understand her, and he yelled in English, "Just drop the claw, lady."

And I couldn't say anything that either of them would understand, so I stared with one unobscured eye as the two of them fought. For a woman her age, Inez was putting up a stunning defense against a college athlete.

An athlete who had, of course, nearly just died of hypothermia.

At one point, she managed to angle the claw against his forearm, dragging a red line down his skin. He grunted, but it had no other effect on him, because of course, Justin didn't possess magic.

He just was who he was. A human being who was trying to protect me.

And the thought hit me like a hammer: Justin knew I wasn't Katrina. He had seen me transform into my true form—the encantado form—and had still decided to save me. He was devoting every bit of his strength to that act.

No man had ever done that.

So I needed to help him. I knew from my time in the cafe bathroom that I wouldn't be able to resume my illusion for at least ten or fifteen minutes, but the floor was slick enough that I could swipe my tail at Inez.

The two of them weren't far from me. After she cut Justin with the claw, he'd backed off a little, and she was moving to sit up.

"Not on my watch," I squeaked, and when her eyes flicked to me, my massive tail swept around and walloped her right in the face. It was the equivalent of getting hit with a really wet towel—not a serious damage-dealer, but enough of a shock to stun a woman in her eighties.

She dropped halfway back, and Justin managed to grab her hand and squeeze the claw out of her grip. He sent it clattering across the floor, and she tried to roll over to reach for it, but by that point he had her fully pinned.

"*Fera!*" She struggled against him. Her dark eyes lit on me with almost feral intensity. "*Você deve destruir a besta. Isso destruiu minha família.*"

"*You must destroy the beast,*" she had said. "*It destroyed my family.*"

"I don't know what you're saying," Justin said, "but it's over. You're not going to get her."

I blinked, stared at him. He meant me. I was a *her*—not a beast. Not a monster.

I had a gender.

And because I couldn't say or do anything else on that kitchen floor until my magic returned, I wept.

↔

Twenty minutes later, I sat on one of the kitchen chairs, huddled in a blanket. Across from me sat Inez, who had been reduced to staring, her hands bound with curtain ties to the chair Justin had sat her on.

Justin stood between us, his own blanket wrapped around his lower half like a Greek statue who'd just stepped out of the shower. Somehow, bedraggled and exhausted as he was, he had never looked more attractive.

"So," he said to me, "who are you?"

I swallowed, pushed my curly red hair over my shoulder. I hadn't resumed my Katrina illusion; this time I'd gone back to my original appearance, the one everyone else knew me as. "Isabella Ramirez," I whispered. "I'm an Other. A student here at McGill."

He studied my face. "You do look kind of familiar."

"I live two doors down from Katrina."

He made gun-fingers at me, like we weren't in the apartment of a woman who'd just tried to kill me. Evidently he'd been through a lot of stressful situations with Kat. "That's it."

But he didn't smile.

"Você vai queimar," came the hissed words.

My gaze flicked down to Inez, whose bloodshot eyes narrowed on me. She hadn't spoken in English since the tussle. "All the hells are gone," I murmured.

"What did she say?" Justin asked.

"She said I would burn."

"Whatever replace Hell will have you." Her voice sounded flinty, defiant. Any elegance her hair might have possessed had disappeared during the struggle, and it now lay tangled and half-matted around her face.

For the first time, I allowed myself to stare at her. At the smoker's lines threaded around her lips, and at the grooves between her eyebrows. She bore nothing of happiness on her face—no laugh lines, no crow's feet.

"How long did you say you've waited to find me?" I said in Portuguese.

"Seventy years," she spat. "Since I was a girl."

"Seventy years," I whispered. "You spent your whole life seeking revenge for your father. Why didn't you come for me before I left Brazil?"

"I could never find you." Her eyes glazed as she remembered. "Not until the curse—until I was taught to summon the creature."

El Lobizon.

"And you followed me here to Canada. How did you know I was here?"

"The creature led me. It scented you on my father's shirt, and when you used your magic ..."

She meant when I'd used my magic on arrival in Montreal, I realized. That had occurred over a year ago. She'd traveled all the way from Brazil to Canada, and only now had she found me. Now that I'd used my magic a second time, to transform into Katrina Darling.

My eyes widened. "After all those decades, it scented my magic on his clothing?"

She didn't answer, but her thin lips came together hard.

"Inez, were you ever married? Did you have children?"

She didn't respond to this, either, but her eyes blazed with ire. *It isn't just me she hates,* I realized. *It's the life she's lived.*

I stood from the chair, crossed to where Inez sat. I knelt in front of her so that she had to look down on me. "I'm sure your father was many wonderful things, Inez, but here's the truth: he wasn't the man you believed him to be."

"Enganador," she breathed, jerking against her restraints like she would bite me.

I straightened, and behind me I heard Justin step forward. "What did she say?"

I raised one staying hand. "She called me a deceiver." Then I spoke in Portuguese. "Inez, your father was a man who abandoned his family for an illusion, and when he discovered the truth of that illusion—of me—he abandoned me, too. He called me a monster, and left me."

"So he saw you for what you are."

"For my part," I continued, "I didn't know you existed. And I can't say whether I would have let him be even if I had. I only knew I loved him unconditionally, unendingly."

She didn't speak, but tears rose in her eyes. Of rage? Of sorrow? I didn't know.

"I know you hate me too much to believe anything I tell you," I said. "But I see your suffering all over your face. A life lived for revenge isn't a life at all."

Inez screwed up her mouth and spat. It landed on my cheek, and I jerked back, one hand rising to my face. She stared at me with shaking anger, the kind of anger that ceases to be about anything except what exists inside.

It wasn't even me she hated anymore. It was just hate.

Under the blanket, one of my hands went to my neck, searching out my amulet. But it wasn't there.

"All right, that's enough," Justin said, stepping forward.

I rose, wiping Inez's spit from my cheek. "Where's my amulet?" I stepped around the kitchen table, scanning the floor.

"Your what?" Justin asked.

"The necklace I always wore." It had never left my neck since the gods departed, not even when I changed illusions. Not even when I entered encantado form. It was bound to me, the one possession I couldn't lose.

Justin knelt, and I heard a tinkling as the emerald gem rose into view, hitting the light with a single, blinding flash. "It slid under the refrigerator."

I crossed to him, lifted it slowly from his fingers. I rubbed the gem, which swirled under the light. "The second life," my sister Ananda had called it when she gave it to me. Her precious amulet—her greatest treasure. She'd put it into my hands when we encantados became mortal, just after the gods departed.

"I don't need it anymore," she'd said. "Not where I'm going."

"Where is that?" I asked.

She winked. "Las Vegas."

She called it a last illusion that wasn't an illusion at all, but the most powerful magic still available in the world. I had worn it around my neck ever since. And I had been instructed to safeguard it until my end.

This wasn't my end, but I understood now what I had been safeguarding it for.

I swicked open one of the drawers in the kitchen, found a series of utensils in a tray. I grabbed up the sharpest knife I could find and turned back to Inez.

"What are you doing, Isabella?" Justin asked.

I walked across the tiles toward Inez, the amulet in one hand and the knife in the other. "The right thing."

"What is this?" Inez said as I placed the chain over her head, the amulet settling on her chest. She breathed faster with the pressure of the amulet on her. "Witch! Curse you."

I got on my knees in front of her, gripped the knife so that the end of it pointed right at the amulet's heart—right at Inez's heart—and took a quick breath. "It's the end of this life," I whispered in Portuguese, "and the beginning of another."

For both her and me.

With that, I stabbed the point into the heart-center of the amulet.

↔

"Isabella, stop!" Justin yelled. His arms swept around me. But it was done. The amulet's magic had been released, and it swirled around us now in streaks of forest green.

The forests of my home. Of the Amazon rainforest.

Inez screamed as the magic enveloped her, cloaking her like many ribbons wrapped around and around and around as she spewed English and Portuguese words into the air: "Demon! *Magia odiosa!* Stop this—stop it!"

I allowed Justin to pull me back, the knife slipping from between my fingers and hitting the tile as the ribbons obscured Inez completely, from head to toes.

Soon, I couldn't even hear her voice anymore.

"What's happening?" Justin said, his arms still around me. So strong, so steady.

"You'll see," I whispered, my eyes filling. I swiped at them with the blanket's edge; I didn't want to miss this.

We watched in silence as the ribbons tightened to Inez's form, and then all at once they wound themselves away, slipping to the ground and dissipating as they touched the tiles.

First her face. Then her chest and arms. Then the rest of her, like a painting. Like a dream.

"Holy … " Justin murmured.

Like her father, Inez had been beautiful. Would be again, for the rest of her life. Her long life.

She blinked, lowered her eyes. Black hair ran in rivulets over her shoulders and down her chest. "What have you done," she breathed, and the voice that issued into the small kitchen didn't have the creakiness I'd come to know, but a softness. Youthfulness.

I pressed against Justin's hold, and he allowed me to slip out. I came toward Inez, who stared at me with the wide-eyed uncertainty she must have borne as a young woman. Her father's same wide-eyed gaze.

Those green eyes glittered as I untied her hands, one and the next. She didn't spit on me. She didn't yell. She only lifted her hands, turned them over. And back again. Brought them to her hair, her face.

"Porque?" she said.

I set one hand on the back of her head like an ordaining. "I'm sorry, Inez. For your mother. For your father. And for the seventy years you spent seeking revenge. This time, you can spend them in joy instead of fear."

Because that was the true root of all anger, all hatred: just fear.

And for my part, I didn't feel so afraid anymore.

She stood, crossed to stare at her blurred reflection on the stove-top. For a minute, no one spoke. Not until Inez did.

"You know," she said in Portuguese, gripping the stove's edges and staring into it like a pond, "I don't even remember his face. I was too young to remember what he was really like."

"He was dark-haired and handsome," I said. "As much as you are beautiful."

She turned toward me, her face angled up to meet my eyes. And for one moment, I couldn't speak. She looked so much like the man I had once loved, and once you truly love someone, seeing them again —even their likeness—can still floor you.

"Is this real?" she whispered. "It's another trick—a dream, a—"

I shook my head, took a deep breath. "It's magic, but it's no trick. This is my gift to you."

"Why?" she said again.

"Because you lost your father, and no matter what he was to me, he was your god. Losing your god changes everything."

Tears filled her eyes. She lowered her forehead to the countertop and wept with her arms crossed over her head. She sobbed as if she was alone, unselfconsciously.

I knew it was time for us to go. My eyes rose to Justin, and I extended my hand toward him between the folds of the blanket. Something floated high in my chest as he touched my hand, and the two of us walked into the living room and found our clothes and shoes laid on the floor.

Justin lifted his jeans. "They're too wet to wear."

"Just the shoes, then," I said, pulling on my boots.

He did the same, and the two of us stepped out of the silent apartment and into the frigid night.

We closed the door behind us, stood facing onto the street for a few seconds.

"Well," I said. Now the barrage of questions would begin. What was all that? Where did she come from? Why was she trying to kill you? And just the thought of them lidded my eyes, made me feel exhausted.

"We're naked," Justin said.

I glanced over at him, pulling my blanket tighter around me. He didn't say anything else. I suppressed a smile. "Nothing you haven't seen before."

He let a small exhale of amusement, the first good feeling I'd managed to elicit from him as Isabella. As me—not Kat.

His eyes traveled up and down the road. "I know where we are. It's about ten minutes from the O³ house." Then his gaze came back to me. "What should we do about her?"

"Inez?" I shook my head. "Nothing."

"She tried to kill you. She summoned a massive were-dog thing."

"It's over." I revealed El Lobizon's claw from the folds of my blanket. It glimmered, iridescent in the moonlight. "El Lobizon won't be hunting us anymore."

And I knew it to be true.

I lifted my eyes; for how cold Montreal was, the city certainly had its appeal. As a Brazilian—used to forests and temperate nights—that wasn't easy to admit.

Justin's voice interrupted the drift of my thoughts. "What will you do with that thing?"

I returned my eyes to the claw. "I'll keep it. As a reminder of who I've been, and who I want to be."

"And who do you want to be?"

I adjusted the claw under the moonlight, watched the colors play across it. "Still me, but the better part. The part of me who makes choices I can stick by. Do you know what I mean?"

"Yes," he said. "I think I do."

"You *think* you do?"

"Well, we've only just met."

Touche.

"We should walk back to my place together, just to be safe."

My eyebrows lifted as I turned to him. "Your place? You don't hate me?"

He shook his head. "Hate? I've never hated anyone. I mean, you did trick me into believing you were my girlfriend, which was a terrible thing to do. And I nearly died ... twice."

I lowered my eyes. "Yes."

His hand came out, the warm fingers finding mine. "But you also saved my life in the river. You gave that woman an incredible gift. You were brave tonight, Isabella."

"I'm an Other. An encantado. My true form is ..."

"Is ...?"

"Terrible. Ugly."

I felt him shrug. "So you're a pink mer-dolphin when you aren't a beautiful young woman. Trust me, I've seen weirder Others since I came to McGill."

I raised my face, trying to keep my chin from crumpling. "Really?"

"Oh yeah. You should meet Mergen; he either looks like the Stay Puft Marshmallow Man or a translucent scarecrow."

I laughed a little, wiped my eyes. All I wanted right now was to stay by Justin's side, to hold his hand, to climb into the same bed as him. And maybe those things were possible. But just because they were possible didn't mean I had to rush them along. We'd both nearly died, and we needed sleep. Food. Warmth. And we had time for those things. I didn't have to pretend I was someone else anymore; the illusions between us had fallen like a veil.

Plus, there was the real Katrina. Still out there, somewhere.

I took a long breath before I smiled up at him. "Thank you for the offer to walk back together. But I'm going to head back to my dorm tonight."

"Okay," he said with a little surprise. He squeezed my hand before turning away, but I held on.

"Justin," I said.

He glanced back.

My thumb rubbed once over the back of his hand. "See you around?"

He nodded, a curl forming at the side of his mouth. "See you around, Isabella."

I started toward my dorm, the claw clutched in my hand. As I walked, a bird screeched through the night once. *It's just a bird, Isa,* I thought, because I had nearly cleared a foot off the ground.

But I still jogged the rest of the way back to the dorm, and not just because it was cold.

CHAPTER TWELVE

$\mathcal{W}$hen I closed my eyes, I saw him. The wolf—the hunter. He'd been behind my eyelids all week.

I lifted my head, turned toward Aimee on the bed next to me. "Did you shower today? You might have my scent on you."

She lifted her own head, eyes lidded as she let a puff of smoke into the air. "Isa, this is my last joint, and I'm not going to waste this afternoon obsessing over the past."

The past, I repeated. *The past.* I lowered my head, let out a long sigh against the current of my thoughts. It didn't matter if she had my scent on her—the hunter was gone. He was in the past. "Sorry."

"Usually I'm the paranoid one."

She was right; we'd reversed roles. Which was strange, because a little weed had almost never made me paranoid like this. And I had been high many, many times—chalk it up to five hundred years of immortality and a whole lot of natural curiosity.

Then again, a week ago I had survived a vengeful Brazilian stalker and her supernatural wolf, all of which had resulted in just barely surviving a dip in a frozen river. That kind of experience rewired the circuitry of your brain.

I hadn't seen Inez since. I took that as a good sign—the best possible sign: she was enjoying her new (youthful) life. Or, at least, not trying to kill me anymore.

Next to me, Aimee's hand found mine. "Just be in the moment. Tell me what you see."

I lifted my eyes. Above us, the dorm room swirled. "It's a storm," I said, nearly dropping the bud as I propped up on my elbows. I reached up from where I lay on my bed, fingers tracing through the air.

"No"—Aimee plucked the blunt from between my fingers and raised it to her mouth—"it's the ocean." She set it to her lips, inhaled.

"That's beautiful," I whispered, the paranoia ebbing. I flopped onto my stomach, pressing aside the wrappers on my duvet. "Hey." I lifted one wrapper, then another, and a third, finding each empty. "You ate it."

Aimee blinked once as she raised the bud from her mouth, and with it, offered a new stream of white smoke to the ocean on our ceiling. "Ate what?"

I crumpled the wrapper I held. "The last Twinkie."

She gasped. "You accuse me?" She struggled to her elbows, half-lidded eyes searching out my own. "I've only had one to your six."

As she sat up, I spotted a glint on the bed. I shoved her aside. "Hey!" she yelped, but I'd already snatched the flattened mass of dough and cream from beneath her. "Chill out, Stay Puft."

I still didn't know who Stay Puft was; I held the treat to my chest. "You were hiding it."

She huffed and dropped onto her back. "I'll never understand Others and their obsessions with junk food. It's not like you never had access to that stuff."

"It's not junk," I said. "If you had lived five hundred years before the mass production of refined sugar, you would understand." I tugged the plastic with pinched fingers. It came apart with machine-perfect exactness, and the aroma of porous dough and cream touched my nose. I stared at the Twinkie before me. The last one.

Aimee caught my eye. "What is it?"

I held it out between us, an offering to the GoneGods. "Do you think eating this is the equivalent of burning a little time?"

84

She stared at me, her blue eyes widening. "That would mean ..."

I waited, the delicacy still held out between us. I started into a slight nod; whatever Aimee was about to say would be profound, important.

"That would mean the entire food industry has been designed around forcing us to burn time."

I nodded harder.

She sat up. "Sugar. It's in everything. Absolutely everything."

I pushed half the Twinkie out of the wrapper and bit it off, nodding still.

Somewhere under the pile of covers, a chirping sounded. We stared at each other, both perplexed. It sounded again.

"Isa, I think a bird flew in."

I threw the covers aside, wrappers flying with them, and uncovered the source. I lifted my phone, blinking hard at the unfamiliar number on the screen. "No bird," I murmured, and all at once, I couldn't remember what time it was. How long had we been here? I accepted the call. "Hello?"

"Isabella?" came a man's voice.

"Is that your new hot thing calling?" Aimee asked, leaning close. "Justin, is that you?"

I set a hand on her face, palm atop her nose, and pushed her back. My head swam, and I sat up on the bed to keep myself still. "Professor Allman?"

"I'm sorry to be calling so late," he said. He spoke almost too fast for me to follow. "I've got huge news. It's about your genetics research."

"My genetics research," I repeated, the details of my own life returning to me from the haze. "On Other DNA?"

"Yes," he said. "Isabella, you've received a huge grant. Well, the whole biology department, but they've earmarked most of it for your work."

I pressed Twinkie crumbs off my mouth with the back of my hand. "No shit. I mean—sorry, Professor. Why my work? I'm just an undergraduate."

He laughed a little. "To be honest, Isa, I had the same reaction. As you know, we have a whole host of graduate students and professors doing important work here. But they were very specific about supporting your gene-mapping project."

That was strange; reactions to my Other gene mapping efforts had been mostly received with indifference, if not occasional derision. The truth was, even at an open-minded place like McGill, most people still placed a priority on Homo sapiens. Not many cared all that much about Others, much less their DNA. Only the military had ever shown interest in the makeup of Others, while universities—and more specifically, science departments—considered our kind so foreign, our biologies were considered almost indistinguishable from magic.

Of course, magic is science unexplained. Being an Other, I could see patterns that escaped human scientists' minds. Not that it mattered—almost every paper I'd put forth in my three semesters was dismissed as fiction. *Seres humanos estúpidos.*

"Who's 'they'?" I asked.

A pause. Stoned as I was, I sensed a weight on the other end of the line. "The Other Anti-Extinction Initiative."

Aimee, whose head was pressed alongside mine, shot me a confused glance, which I returned. "Who?" she whispered.

"Isabella," Professor Allman asked, "are you alone?"

"I'm in my dorm with my roommate." *And 100% not high.*

"I think it'd be best if you just came in to my office tomorrow so we can discuss this. It's good news—great news, so you should be happy. But it'll mean changes."

Changes. He'd delivered that word with none of his typical enthusiasm.

A knock sounded at the door. *Tap-ta-tap-tap.* Justin's knock. Then his muffled voice: "Isabella?"

He was early. *Two hours* early.

My stomach slid over, and I rose, pressing wrappers and crumbs off my shirt. "What time tomorrow?" I said into the phone.

"Noon. And be prepared for company, okay?"

Aimee was already sashaying to the door. "I'll get it," she called.

Aimee was never this loud, this extroverted. GoneGodDamn, how high had we gotten?

"I'll be there, Professor," I said, ending the call and making a dash for the mirror—my eyes looked redder than a black cadejo—while flapping my hands at Aimee, who saw none of what I was doing, both hands trying to yank the door open.

"This door is broken," she said.

"It's a turn knob." I pushed my red hair away from my face, disentangling a glob of something yellow. Cheese? Yes, it was cheese. When had we eaten—

"Justin!" Aimee called, throwing her arms into the air. "Isa, it's your *namorado*." She had been taking Portuguese 101, and somehow she'd already learned the word *boyfriend*.

"*Ele não é meu namorado*," I chided, leaning to see past her. There he stood in the doorway: the man I'd fallen not-so-secretly in love with, tall and black-haired and staring right at me with a look in his eyes I'd seen before.

Admiration. Desire. Affection.

And he was looking at me, plain Isabella. I looked like myself now —at least, the Isabella I'd been when I came to McGill: red-haired, green-eyed, freckled and average height.

It was an amazing feeling.

But the better feeling—the one I'd never expected—was to care so much about a man who knew I was an encantado and looked at me like that anyway. I felt like a deer caught in a pair of headlamps. In the best way.

Except something in Justin's expression suggested trouble, despite the half-smile he'd conjured. He coughed, one hand sweeping through the air. "You two are going to set off the smoke alarm."

"It's been a good night," Aimee said. "And it's about to get *muito quente*."

Now I felt myself blushing, especially when Justin's lips curled. "This is an unexpected surprise. You're two hours early."

"Are you here for *beijos*?" Aimee grinning up at him. "*Muitos beijos?*"

What are *beijos*?" Justin asked.

"Aimee," I rasped, "shut up."

He ruffled his hand through his hair. "Sorry to surprise you." He stepped into the room, letting the door shut behind him. "It's just, I'm not sure if it's a good idea for you to be out alone at night."

I made a face. Was Justin a secret chauvinist? "I'll have you know that I'm perfectly capable—"

My phone began vibrating in my hand. Aimee's did the same on her desk. I lifted mine. CAMPUS ALERT, the screen read. UNCOMMON CONCENTRATION OF BIRDS FLOCKING ON CAMPUS. DO NOT AGGRAVATE OR INTERACT WITH FLOCKS.

"Uh," Aimee said from her desk. "What?"

"Yeah, it's kind of weird," Justin said. "And in my experience, when things get weird, they get dangerous."

"This is a joke." I crossed to the window. Outside, the setting sun streaked through the clouds and an otherwise bare sky. No birds. "It's the middle of winter—they shouldn't be flocking at all. It's not the students who should be concerned … it's bird conservationists."

"Maybe it's best if we don't go out tonight," Justin said. "To be safe."

I kept staring out the window, and I realized that I hadn't left my dorm all week except to attend class. I'd spent the whole time vaguely traumatized, paranoid about what had happened.

But it's in the past.

"No." I turned. "I want to go out tonight. To celebrate."

Justin's eyebrows went up.

I half-smiled. "My research just got a huge grant."

Justin threw his hands up, and so did Aimee, and the two of them came at me at once and despite my objections, I was soon enveloped by four human arms. "That's amazing," Justin said. "All right, the two of you get on your coats."

"No way," Aimee said. "I'm not getting in the middle of this."

I shot her a glare. "Aimee, we're not—"

"Dating?" She scoffed, broke away and dropped back onto the bed. "Whatever. That's why you two are still pressed against each other."

I glanced down; Justin's arms were wrapped low around my waist, and mine were clasped at the back of his neck. I stepped back, and I sensed his unwillingness to let me go, even though I knew he was conflicted about Katrina and me.

The thing is, throughout history we encantados have been great "breaker-uppers." In fact, you could call us the royalty of broken relationships. This time, I was trying to be better than that. I wanted to do this right.

But then I saw that jaguar's grin spread across his features, and I thought, *Better, but I'm not going for sainthood.*

"I need to get ready. My eyes slowly tracked up to Justin's; sometimes gazing at him felt like looking into the sun. "Meet me at the street corner like we talked about?"

"Are you sure?"

I set one finger at the center of his chest, and he swallowed, his Adam's apple bobbing hard. The encantado effect. "Don't worry—I know how to take care of myself."

CHAPTER THIRTEEN

*a*s I walked to St. Catherine Street to meet up with Justin, I crossed by the river.

The surface bore a thick layer of ice. Atop it rested a foot of untouched snow.

I stood for a few minutes at its edge, hands in my pockets, and stared at the spot where I'd broken through a week ago. As several hundred years of immortality had taught me, nature worked fast. You couldn't even tell, much less have guessed—if you weren't me, Justin or my roommate Aimee—what lay beneath.

The hunter. El Lobizon.

He'd frozen there, claws outstretched toward me in his last moment of majesty. When it warmed, would he be washed away with the breaking ice? Or perhaps he'd vanished already, disappeared into the ether from which he'd been summoned.

Either way, I had returned to this spot every day since. I felt somehow dutybound to keep vigil. And I'd kept a token from our battle: his massive claw, which rested in my purse. Hey, a dagger that can also nullify magic? Way better than a mace.

But the claw was more than that, I thought as I walked toward our meeting spot downtown. It also represented the first time in my life I hadn't run away. And as I stood at the corner of St. Catherine under the streetlamp, that knowledge warmed me despite the frigid January air.

"You're awfully cute with red hair."

Delicious pride filled me; I knew that voice was referring to me, Isabella Ramirez, and no one else. My lips curled, and I spun on my heels, shrugging with my hands deep in my coat pockets. "You're lucky *you're* so cute, or else I'd be supremely irritated by your lateness."

There stood Justin Truly. Every time I heard that voice, spotted those blue eyes and black hair, I wondered at how the gods could have justified gracing one man with so much charm before they left.

"Hey," he said, palms going up, "I was the one who came by your dorm extra early."

"And unexpectedly."

We came together on the sidewalk, he staring down and I up until our bodies nearly touched. My hands didn't leave my pockets. "Tell me meeting here wasn't worth it."

I knew from the look in his eyes how I appeared to him: a beautiful stranger standing on the street. And it was this string of tension —the little surprises, the unexpectedness—that would make the culmination of what was happening between us explosive. Eventually. When the time was right.

He nodded once, eyes unwavering. "It was worth it."

I stepped beside him, sliding my hand through the crook of his arm. "I hope you like greasy spoons."

"What, like a diner? Are we ... going steady? Like two teenagers from the fifties?"

"I'll have you know, that was a particularly good decade." We started down the sidewalk, the setting sun pale on us through the clouds. I still hadn't seen any dangerous flocks of birds since we'd received a campus alert about them earlier that afternoon. "And no, we're not going steady. We're celebrating my research getting funded," I deflected.

I knew what he was asking, but Justin was with Katrina—who still hadn't appeared since the semester began—and he and I were dancing around this thing between us, unwilling to name it and equally unwilling to ignore it.

After all, a week ago I'd hoodwinked him into thinking I was his absentee girlfriend, Kat—which is a long story. But the gist is: if you were an encantado with the ability to look like anyone, and your love interest's girlfriend hadn't shown her face in weeks, wouldn't you burn two months off the end of your life to look like her for a while?

We'd sort of gotten past it, but we still had to get to know each other better now that I looked like me. Well, he had to get to know *me* better—the real Isabella. And he had to choose between Kat and me.

"Justin," I said, "what we're doing isn't as innocent as you make it out to be."

We passed a few other groups of pedestrians, turned at a cross street that would take us toward the restaurant I'd picked. As soon as we did, the street noise grew.

"I don't know what you mean," Justin said. But he avoided meeting my eyes for the first time since we'd met up.

"You asked me if we're going steady. You can't fool a 500-year-old encantado—I know *all* the signs."

He pretended to be distracted by a storefront display of candles. "Signs of what?"

"Of when a man is considering cheating on his significant other."

He slowly unhooked his arm from mine. That was never good. "I'm not a cheater," he said in a low, testy voice.

I stepped ahead of him, turned so we were facing. When I put my hands on his arms, he stopped and looked down at me. "I know that," I said. "But all this time we're spending together … it's only going to hurt your relationship with Kat."

He took a deep breath. "My relationship with Kat is pretty hurt already."

"What do you mean?"

"We had a big falling out before winter break. I haven't even talked to her since then, and I don't know if she wants to be with me or not. And then you showed up."

"Which is why you were asking me why I hadn't called or texted when I showed up in the dining hall that day, pretending to be Kat."

He nodded.

It was all making more sense now.

"You and she need to talk," I said.

"We will—once I can get in touch with her."

"And you need to decide who you want to be with."

Some small, egocentric part of me hoped he'd say, *"You. I want to be with you."* But the larger part of me was glad when he said, "I will. I won't keep you in the dark—I promise."

Because that was what rational, responsible people did. Even if they sometimes made the irresponsible choice to hang out with women they were clearly attracted to.

"OK," I said. "So do you want to go to this diner? As friends."

He smiled at me. "You're the best-looking friend I've ever had. Every guy we've passed has been staring." He said it so smoothly I couldn't help but laugh, and the thought occurred to me that I hadn't gone a day without seeing his face since that night we'd jumped into the river, and maybe I didn't want to.

"It's an encantado thing," I said as we resumed walking. "Besides, the *women* we passed certainly weren't staring at me."

Before we reached the curb, Justin's body tensed, and he slowed us. "Isa," he said, "what is that?"

"What is what?" I began.

Then I saw it. Correct that: everyone on the sidewalk saw it. And just as the first street lamp illuminated, the screaming started.

↔

Above us, the sky churned black. Black with birds.

Darting, diving, sparks spraying from their bodies like flint on tinder. Together, their screeching radiated into the center of my brain, and my hands clapped to my ears. But the damage had already been done; my ears rang, my head pounded, and I vaguely recognized one of them breaking off from the flock, diving toward us talons-first, enormous wings outstretched.

Justin yanked me back, the air displacing in front of my face as I stumbled. A quick *thwack thwack* sounded to our left, and the little compact car parked on the curb rocked on its frame. Two impossibly unbroken feathers were sunk halfway into the passenger-side door.

The 100% metal door.

The bird circled back around, rejoining the swirling mass. The screeching continued, but by now it was muffled by the awful ringing in my head.

Justin pulled me to him, and we fell against the brick wall of a building. "Are you OK?"

I blinked up at him. He sounded so far away. "That bird just shot metal feathers at me."

As a native of the Brazilian rainforests, I could identify just about any bird in South America with one glance. And I'd carried that interest with me to Canada; I'd spent many hours in the library studying bird species native to North America, not least because Professor Allman loved the creatures of that continent, too. We'd spent hours chatting about different species.

So I was kind of obsessed with birds, OK? Hundreds of years spent in nature will have that effect.

But I had no idea what I'd just seen. They were avian creatures, but it was like we'd stepped onto the set of a Hitchcock film. Above us, a thick flock of them obscured the sky, their metallic wings glinting in the light as they dove at the fleeing pedestrians.

Half a block away, a man raised his arm against one of the dive-bombers, and it shredded his coat from wrist to shoulder with its beak.

Elsewhere, people sprinted to get indoors as feathers peppered the cars like hail and stop signs and the brick facades of the buildings. And even brick wasn't strong enough to withstand the feathers, which hit the stone and remained jutting at whatever angle they had been launched from.

And Justin? He was on his phone.

"St. Catherine Street," he was saying. I could barely hear his voice over all the noise. "An entire flock of birds. Metal feathers. They seem to be Others."

"Who the hell are you talking to?" I said. "Because now isn't the best time."

Justin ignored me. "Yes, sir. I'll take care." When he hung up, he stepped in front of me, shielding me with his body. "We have to get out of here—now."

"Exactly what I was thinking." But first, I spun toward the lacerated car.

"Isa, what are you doing?"

I knelt by the wings lodged into the door, raising my fingers to the top one. It reflected the chaos behind me, glimmered under the artificial lamp above us. I just barely brushed my finger over its edge; it felt like a perfectly sharpened knife.

The feathers really were made of metal.

Justin's hands clamped around my sides, pulling me up. "I'm sorry to say we don't have time for that, Biologist."

I resisted, grabbing the door's latch. As I did, the car's alarm went off, adding to the cacophony on the street. "Wait! I need one of these feathers," I said. "Help me get it out."

He gave me a look I was starting to become familiar with: pure exasperation. But then he yanked off his coat. "I'll get it," he said. "Just get behind the car."

I did as he said, ducking in front of its hood. I watched as, with amazing quickness, he wrapped the coat around the lodged feather, set one boot against the door, and yanked it straight out. The golden tip came free like a dagger, and Justin the hero out of some Arthurian legend.

Then the window shattered next to him—a trio of deadly feathers launched by one of the diving birds—and I was brought back to the reality of our situation. We were just a human and an Other, and I had put him at enormous risk.

When he dashed around the car and dropped next to me, he passed the feather over, still wrapped in his coat. "Why do you need this, anyway?" he yelled over all the noise.

I glanced up at the sky; the flock had shifted. Where a minute ago it had circled a block away, it seemed to be moving in our direction. "I'll tell you later," I yelled back, bundling it under my arm and grabbing his hand. I pointed at a bookstore just across the street from us, only about twenty feet away. When our eyes met, he nodded.

The two of us leapt up, running across the street with our hands still locked. He moved faster, of course—one of the few times I regretted choosing a five-foot-three illusion—and I nearly tripped to keep up with him.

The screeching hadn't stopped, but by now, it had become part of my world. I couldn't hear anything else—not our footsteps or my own breathing. Only the cries of birds and people.

I certainly loved books, but right now that little bookstore with its twinkle lights looked like an oasis in a desert. We made the sidewalk, and as Justin grabbed the handle and the door belled, I heard a scream unlike any I'd heard since the fracas began. It came from far away, and it didn't sound like a bird or a human.

And the thought hit me as we slipped through the door and into the bookshop:

If death were a sound, I've just heard it.

The door belled once more as it closed behind us, and we were enveloped by silence. Four people stood not far off, one of them the man whose coat sleeve had been shorn from wrist to armpit. It now hung like a drapery off his body, and he cradled his arm to him as he stared at us.

No—past us. At the scene outside.

"Get away from the windows," he said, and Justin and I ducked by instinct as we made for the nearest of the tall bookcases.

"Are you OK?" I heard Justin ask him.

"I'm fine. It just got my jacket."

And in my daze, some part of me processed the curiousness of such a thing as I watched the streets empty ahead of the flock. Clearly those weren't normal birds—I still held a metal feather under my arm, after all—and the one I had seen attack the man next to us could easily have destroyed him with one well-shot feather. Or its beak.

But it hadn't.

And over the next minute, Justin and I and the other four stood there and watched through the picture window as the flock slowly dissipated. Like a sudden storm, violent and intense, before it tapered to nothing.

To silence.

Outside, only the single car alarm I had set off still blared.

"Where in the world did they all come from?" a woman said. She stood behind the counter, palms on its edge.

"I don't know," the man with the shredded jacket began. "My wife and I were walking down the street, and there was an awful screeching. And then they just … appeared all at once."

Justin squeezed my arm before he started toward the door. "They've cleared. We should check to see if anyone's hurt."

My hand went out in his wake; I already missed his closeness.

"You shouldn't. They could still be out there," the woman behind the counter said.

"It's OK," Justin said, hand on the door's handle. "I'm part of the Army cadets."

I blinked. The Army? Did he mean the *World* Army? I mean, he had asked me what I thought about that World Army training poster over a week back, but it had seemed like an offhanded thing. He hadn't mentioned actually joining them in all the times I'd seen him since.

The World Army, from what I knew about it, didn't favor Others. It was, in fact, Otherist in the extreme. Had Justin actually signed up with them? But I didn't have time to ask, because he had already slipped through the door.

I started after him, emerging onto the sidewalk at a jog. "Wait up."

Justin stopped. "It's not safe, Isa."

"They're gone." Though I could still hear that scream echoing deep in my head—the sound of death. The memory of it sent a shiver through me, and I went up to Justin's side. "Besides, safe or not, you're not going anywhere without me."

He sighed, nodded. "OK."

We continued down the street together, the whole of which was lit with feathers like icicles glittering in the night. People were starting to appear from the buildings they had ducked inside, their eyes wide, faces upturned. But only the moon greeted us now, a white orb low in the sky.

When we had walked three blocks, something caught my eye down an alley. I stopped us. "Wait," I said, squinting. "Is that a person?"

Justin and I stood at the mouth of the alley, the whole of which was lit by nothing but the moon. And that was enough to make out the dark edges of what sat slumped against the edge of a metal trash receptacle.

As we neared, my hand went to my mouth.

A young blond man lay before us, a hole where his heart should have been.

CHAPTER FOURTEEN

*T*wenty minutes later, the police arrived. Justin had called them, introducing himself on the phone as a "cadet," though my mind slipped past that unpleasant fact and returned at once to the far more immediate fact of the murder scene. The death.

Justin and I stood six feet apart on the sidewalk, each of us talking to a police officer. And though we'd backed out around the corner from the alley where the young man lay, I couldn't stop glancing at the hard edge of the building as though I might glimpse him. As though I might see again that spot of brick wall visible through the center of his body.

Even with closed eyes, I still saw the agony on his face.

We had been the first ones to discover him, but we didn't know anything more than what we'd seen: a body against a wall. Since then, he'd been surrounded by yellow tape, a white cloth slipped over his body.

The officer, who'd introduced himself as Tremblay, asked me about the birds that had attacked—apparently not a single death had occurred as a result of the flock—and the metal feathers they'd shot off. The one Justin had retrieved for me was still tucked into my coat.

"Based on what you saw, do you believe they're monsters?"

Tremblay asked. He glanced up from his notepad, those perfectly human eyes studying me. He bore a certain crow-footed kindness around the eyes, a little paunch, some wispy white hair near his ears.

"I believe they're Others," I said. "They weren't like any regular bird."

"Right." His pen moved across the paper. And I realized that he didn't make any distinction between monsters and Others. It was as though I'd said only, *"Yes."*

"The reason why I think they're Others and not monsters," I added, "is because they didn't kill or badly injure anyone when they could easily have done so."

Tremblay's eyes lifted to me. "You don't think they killed that boy in the alley?"

I thought back to the razor beaks, the massive talons, the way they'd dived and flocked and shot those feathers off. Those were hunters—birds of prey. If they'd wanted to, they could have killed at least a half-dozen people in the street and injured as many more.

Besides, ripping out just the heart? That was a monstrous thing.

"No," I said. "I don't think they killed him."

Tremblay studied the information he'd written on his pad. "And you're a biology student at McGill, you said?"

"That's right."

"Are you human?"

This line of questioning seemed ... pointed. And then it occurred to me: we were the first two onto the scene. We were more than sources of information. Justin and I were potential suspects.

"I'm an Other," I said, lowering my voice. My eyes drifted toward Justin, who appeared as cool as ever, gesturing and nodding and buzzing with rapport with the officer he'd just met.

I felt Tremblay stiffen next to me. If everything about him hadn't screamed *human* before, his reaction to finding out my Other status was about as human as it got. "Other? What species?"

"Encantado. From Brazil."

"What's that?"

"We're a … an aquatic species. Our natural form is somewhere between a mermaid and a dolphin."

"So why don't you look like a mermaid-dolphin?" And all at once, those crow's feet didn't seem so kind.

"I'm a shapeshifter." I realized how bad this sounded. "It's in our nature to shapeshift into humans."

"Huh," Tremblay finally said. More scratching of that pen on his pad. "When did you arrive in Canada?"

"One and a half years ago, to attend McGill."

"So, recently. How is your English so good?"

Had he really just asked me that? If I were braver—maybe if I still looked like Katrina, whom I had spent a week masquerading as—I would have flashed him a look. As it was, I only lifted my chin to say, "I've been alive five hundred years. I speak eight languages."

Tremblay kept taking notes, as though speaking to a semi-ancient, octolingual being didn't even merit a raised eyebrow. Three, then five seconds elapsed as Justin and the other officer chattered away. Things seemed to be going much better for him.

"Do you have identification?" I heard Tremblay ask me.

I fished both my Canadian ID card and passport out of my purse, tried to keep my hand from shaking as I passed them over. It was the cold, I wanted to tell him. *Try spending hundreds of years in a rainforest and then acclimate to Canadian winters.* But I found myself saying as little as possible—a protective measure I'd developed around authority figures. And people whom I believed didn't mean well.

And I was starting to suspect Tremblay really didn't mean me well.

He opened the passport, stared. Swapped the ID card to the fore, stared at that. Ten seconds later, he extended both back. "What about your Other ID?"

Merda, my fingers were shaking even more. "Other ID?"

"A new Other requirement," he said, a certain strain of victory echoing in that baritone voice. "All Others in Canada have to carry them, per the World Government."

"Since when?" I said, my rare temper flaring. This was a ridiculous encroachment on Other rights, and I was about to tell him so at great length, in both English and Portuguese, when Justin appeared from nowhere, his warm hand enfolding mine.

"Officer," he said, "I couldn't help but overhear you mentioning the Other ID. I'm a new cadet here on campus, and as it happens, we were just briefed about the ID today."

"Oh?" Tremblay said. He looked displeased about Justin's intrusion, but of course, he'd pooled in so swiftly and easily that it felt only natural for him to be a part of the conversation. I recognized it at once: the halo effect coupled with unblinking daring.

"One of the interesting details we learned: since it just went into effect this month, all Others who entered Canada before January have until July to obtain their ID."

"You're a cadet, you say?"

Justin nodded, that boyish half-smirk appearing on his face. I stared between him and Tremblay, whose crow's feet deepened just a few degrees. GoneGodDamn, why couldn't I do a boyish half-smirk?

"It's good you found the poor kid," Tremblay said, nodding toward the murder scene around the corner. "We need more citizens like you."

And like that, our suspiciousness washed off us as simply as dirt in the shower. But if anything, I felt dirtier than before.

Shame doesn't wash off so easily.

↔

Afterward, Justin stood close to me, and I stepped into his arms. We hugged, and as we did, I felt my phone buzz three times in my purse. "That's a campus alert," he murmured by my ear.

"How do you know?"

"We were briefed on that. Three short vibrations mean an alert."

I nodded, wondering what else he'd been "briefed" on as I lifted my phone out of my purse. Well, he was right. CAMPUS ALERT, the text read. STUDENT MURDERED NEAR CAMPUS, SITUATION STILL RESOLVING. STAY INDOORS UNTIL FURTHER NOTICE.

"What's going on?" I whispered. The birds, the murder. Even Professor Allman's call about my grant funding and "meeting in his office" had seemed mysterious, foreboding. I remembered my happiness of a few hours ago as a simple, faraway thing.

"Whatever it is," Justin said, "I think we should get indoors. One of the officers offered to give us a ride back. We should take it."

"OK," I said, even though the last thing I wanted was to ride with Tremblay, or any other officer. But I felt numbed through.

We climbed into the car and the officer who'd spoken with Justin started toward my dormitory in silence. After a few minutes, Justin's hand squeezed mine. "It was an Other who killed that guy, wasn't it?" He was talking to the officer.

"We really don't know as yet," the officer said. He was being vague because we were civilians, but I sensed he agreed with Justin. I knew from my long history of interacting with humanity that they were capable of doing every depraved thing imaginable to their own species, but since the gods had left, perceptions had changed.

By default, Others were held responsible for such depravity.

And in that moment, I discovered my temper again. "Does it matter?"

Justin's eyes flew to me with a certain surprise. "Absolutely," he said. "If it's an Other, they operate by different rules, protocol, motivations—"

"Right at this moment"—I held his gaze—"does it matter?"

Justin studied me, and after a moment the hardness in his jaw softened. He understood, and his arm came out. I leaned into him, my head on his shoulder. "No," he said. "Right at this moment, it doesn't."

So I still had more sway over him than the World Army's teachings, at least. A small comfort. He didn't speak again until we arrived at my dormitory, but that thing still hung in the air between us ... the stickiness of a wedge, future problems.

After all, I was one of them—the Others, the depraved.

When we arrived at my dorm and I stepped out of the police car, Justin leaned out after me. "Can I see you tomorrow?"

I turned back, pulling my coat tight. "I have a meeting with Professor Allman."

"After?" His pleading blue eyes did 90% of the work. "I'd like to talk about this whole Army cadet thing. I could tell the effect it had on you when I mentioned it."

I sighed, panned my gaze around in the night. The street was unusually empty on account of the alert, and an icy wind hurt my ears and nose. I felt a strong urge to be inside. "After."

"I'll call you."

"Great." I turned away, heard him pull the door closed. Why had I been so brusque? I understood it, in part—he was a cadet for the World Army, an organization whose very mention made me feel a little violated—but it was something bigger.

It had to do with the blackness of the evening. The birds, the murder, the human whose heart had been perfectly carved from his chest. Somewhere nearby lurked a creature capable of such things.

Back in the dorm, Aimee nearly accosted me at the door. "Isa," she cried, clinging to me, "I was so worried about you. I heard about the birds, and then the campus alert about the murder—"

"Woah," I said, stepping away. "Sharp metal object on board." As I pulled from her grasp, I untucked the metallic feather from the recesses of my jacket, the whole of it still wrapped in Justin's coat.

When I revealed it under the fluorescent light, it shone like a piece of glass. As Aimee and I stood over it, our faces reflecting back at us, she opened her mouth. "Is that …?"

"It's a feather."

She reached out, tapped the flat of it with her nail. It made a clinking noise. "OK," she said. "OK. I think we're going to need more weed."

CHAPTER FIFTEEN

$\mathcal{I}$n the night, I dreamed of him. The blond boy missing his heart.

I woke in the early dawn, my own heart thudding so hard against my chest I set a hand there. Through the window, cumulus clouds hung low and gray. And that same blackness pulled at my mind. It pinched with two fingers, wouldn't let go as I dressed, pulled on my coat, set the metallic feather in my purse.

I had six hours until my meeting with Professor Allman. That gave me six hours to figure out what the hell kind of creature this feather had come from.

I clomped down the stairwell as the feeling percolated inside me. Here was the thing, I thought as I stepped into the frigid morning. The birds hadn't killed anyone, even though they could have. And simultaneously, a student had been murdered not two blocks from where they'd flocked.

I inspected the high branches of every tree I passed. Bare, bare, bare, all of them devoid of regular birds, the birds I'd so often hear chirping through my dorm window in the fall, even in the winter.

Even as recently as two days ago.

Around me, the campus spread silent and empty. Normally I'd spot a few early-risers, but not this morning. In fact, I felt more alone than I had since arriving at McGill.

As far as I knew, a suspect still hadn't been brought in for the murder. Which meant he, she—it?—was still walking or crawling or flying. Still at large. And I didn't have a single clue who or what to be looking for, which raised every hair along my spine. And everyone knew that in the scariest movies, not seeing the monster made for an infinitely more frightening time. Because everyone's imagination catered to their own fears, their own scariest monster.

So I just about ran to the Other Studies Library, and when I pushed through the doors, my cheeks had nearly frozen from the wind. I doubled over in the warmth, my purse clutched to my side.

"Oh dear." The librarian at the circulation desk eyed me over her glasses. "What's wrong?"

I straightened, shook my head. "I just got spooked walking here. A student was murdered last night." *And I saw him after he'd died.*

Her aged eyes grew wide. "An awful thing. I heard a few of those World Army cadets found him in the tree."

"No, he was—" I stopped hard. "Wait, what tree?"

"Just outside his dorm, in one of those red ash trees. A sophomore, maybe twenty." The librarian stood, appeared now about to cry as she leaned over the desk toward me. "His eyes were gone. Both of them."

Heart. Eyes. I just stared at her, my body running hot with fresh adrenaline.

"You meant another murder," she realized.

I nodded, both hands on the strap of my purse.

"A student as well?" she asked.

"On Saint Catherine Street," I whispered.

Her eyes reddened, and the librarian slumped back to her seat like she'd been hit in the solar plexus. "What a GoneGodDamned thing." She glanced up at me. "Sorry for cursing, dear."

I waved a hand through the air. When I turned away, started toward the stacks, I realized the noise in my ears from last night had never stopped.

The screeching continued in my head, reduced to a thin ringing.

↔

I got myself together in the bathroom, tried not to look in the mirror. I knew I'd imagine myself eyeless, with a hole in my chest; my imagination was overactive that way.

Twenty minutes later, I flicked on a reading lamp and sat with a stack of books on birds. Given my knowledge of them, it didn't take me long. Birds with metal feathers weren't terribly common throughout history, or in lore. The second book I opened—*Creatures of Greek Mythology*—contained exactly what I'd been looking for.

"Stymphalian," I whispered, finger tracing the lines. Birds of prey, except unlike regular birds, these preferred to eat humans. And they were well-equipped to do so. Beaks and feathers of bronze, the impossibly sharp talons. They had destroyed the ancient countryside like swarms of locusts, devastating crops and villages. And ultimately they had been subdued by Hercules, who had shot them down with arrows tipped in the poisonous blood of the Hydra.

Ancient Greek birds of lore. Where had they come from? And why had they attacked Montreal? And the most baffling part of all: Stymphalian birds were man-eaters, and yet they hadn't killed or eaten any of the slow, sedentary Canadians. Why?

I closed my eyes, both hands set to my face. Last night, it had seemed like they were attacking, but from my studies of birds of prey, I knew they weren't. They had been diverting. Distracting. All that noise, dive-bombing people—it was theater. If they'd been intending to kill, they would have waited for the right moment to swoop in, silent and lethal.

But distracting from what? I stared off into the empty stacks, my ears ringing. Two murders had occurred last night. The heart removed from one victim, the eyes from the other.

What was the story? From everything Justin had told me about his girlfriend, I had a fleeting sense that if I were Katrina Darling, I would be able to piece it all together.

But I wasn't Katrina, and I never would be—even if I'd once looked like her. I was Isabella, and maybe, just maybe this was a problem that didn't need Katrina Darling to solve.

After four hours of research, I pushed the stack of books aside; I needed someone else's mind at work on this, and I knew exactly whose.

I glanced at my watch. By the GoneGods, when had it gotten to be nearly noon? I was going to be late for my meeting. I grabbed up my bag and jogged through the stacks and up to the main floor, passing by the librarian I'd spoken to on my way in.

When I dashed out of the library and came around the corner of the building, I stopped short.

Before me, one of the bare trees on campus was full to the gills with a flock of stymphalian birds, their bronze beaks gleaming in the wisps of light between the clouds. At this distance, I could gauge their true size: as large as pure black cranes, talons longer than my fingers wrapped around the branches. They sat silent, immobile, their dark eyes surveying me from twenty feet away.

I took one step back, my boot barely tapping on the sidewalk. As I did, one of the largest birds jerked to stare at me straight on, its wings parting to reveal a terrifying span, a series of serrated bronze feathers stretching to six feet at either side.

I took another step, not taking my eyes off it, then another. It rose to its full height, legs straightening, and let a screech so tremendous I clapped my hands to my ears, bracing myself. All at once, I felt wind across my body, and I looked up to see the entire flock pulling toward the sky, thirty of them airborne at once.

My lips parted in silent awe as the black cloud swept over and past me, traveling north toward Mont Royal. They hadn't attacked me, and I realized as I watched them disappear over the buildings that I hadn't sensed real malice from them.

Not this time, at least. My eyes lifted to the sun behind the clouds. Were they nocturnal? I hadn't seen any mention of it in the mythology book, but it was, after all, ancient mythology. Another reminder of how, given our newfound coexistence, we knew frighteningly little about Others and monsters. Even I, as an Other, didn't know much about most species of Others.

But right now, I was out of time to ponder stymphalian birds. I ran toward the Stewart Biology building.

Professor Allman's office door was shut. His door was never shut, and right now we were supposed to have a meeting. I knocked, but it didn't open. So I spent five minutes sitting on the tiled floor, my back against the wall. I felt tired, colorless after yesterday, and encountering that flock of stymphalian birds again hadn't helped.

As soon as I closed my eyes, his excited voice echoed down the hall, and a woman's returned. Their shoes clicked on approach, and I pushed myself up the wall. Twenty feet away, a fabulously tall woman in the kind of professional getup I'd thought was the sole realm of magazine models—red heels, black, fitted slacks, an equally black blazer with a white undershirt peeking through—walked in animated conversation with my professor.

When he spotted me, the woman followed his gaze. "Ah, Isabella," Professor Allman said. "Sorry to be late." He wrung his fingers—a gesture I'd become familiar with over the many months we'd spent working together. It was a nervous tic. But this time it was also paired with a faint line of sweat on his brow.

Something about this woman made him nervous.

"This is Isabella?" The woman turned crystal blue eyes on me. I swallowed. Did I ever mention that I prefer men? Well, I'm a bit of an anomaly among encantado, who tend to be equally equally enchanted by both genders. But right now, this woman's hair looked like a black waterfall.

"Yes—the one and only." He gestured between the two of us. "Isabella, this is Dr. Serena Russo, who I've been showing around our research facilities. She'll be the lead scientist on the Other triple helix mapping project, and specifically asked to meet you today. Serena, this is Isabella Ramirez, the undergraduate who's been studying Other DNA since she arrived at McGill, and a brilliant biology student."

It was only when I processed her extended hand that I realized I'd been staring at her hair. "Isabella," she said, and as we shook hands, I didn't even have time to consider all the implications of Dr. Russo's sudden appearance on campus; I was still overwhelmed by her presence. "I'm so much looking forward to working with you on this critically important project."

"You're not a professor here." The thoughtlessness of my statement didn't hit me until I glanced at Professor Allman, whose gray eyebrows had gone up.

Dr. Russo laughed. "No—I'm employed by the Other Anti-Extinction Initiative. As part of the grant afforded to the biology department, I've been asked to head up the research here."

"Serena would very much like to see the work you've been doing, Isabella," Professor Allman's hand touched my back. "If you wouldn't mind showing her now."

"Absolutely." I set both hands on the strap of my purse. I started walking, my eyes glazed. What was the Other Anti-Extinction Initiative, and why did they have so much money to funnel into my work? After all, PR for Others hadn't exactly been great ever since we'd come crashing—as in, some Others had quite literally fallen from the sky when the gods left—into humans' lives.

We came to the lab where I'd been spending half my free time for the past year and a half, and my hands went clammy. Only Professor Allman had really shown any interest in what I'd been doing up until now, and what if he'd only been trying to encourage a naive, short-sighted undergrad? How could I possibly contribute on the level of a woman like Dr. Russo?

We stepped into the lab, and I brought the two of them over to my workstation. "Here it is." I swept an arm out. "All of it."

Dr. Russo stepped forward, surveying the array of equipment. "Tell me what you're trying to do here, Isabella."

I took my deepest breath, set my hands together. Even though I'd spent mountains of time on this work, I hadn't prepared for this moment at all. "As you know, while human DNA forms a double helix,

Other DNA forms a triple helix. I've been attempting to map this strand to gain a better understanding of Other DNA."

"To what end?" Dr. Russo asked.

"It's theorized that the third strand on the helix is what allows Others to tap into magic."

Those blue eyes surveyed my face. "But you don't believe that, do you?"

"No, I believe that when the gods made Others, they used the third strand as a way to mix traits of all of creation into one being. The simplest examples are centaurs, minotaurs and sphinxes—the half-human, half-animal beings." I paused. "But it goes beyond that. A popobawa has spider-like features, but is somehow human, too."

She appeared impressed. "Human? Yes, I've heard the theory. Human emotions, human logic, the human capacity for love, and hate. "

This was my favorite subject, and I couldn't stop myself. "Maybe it's humans who have Other traits. After all, we were created before you."

She chuckled. "I see what Professor Allman meant about you. Sharp, passionate. Determined. But also reserved." Then, "Isabella, what I want is the real reason why you're mapping the Other genome."

"For the same reasons scientists mapped human DNA—to learn more about the species." Though that wasn't exactly true, and I didn't meet Dr. Russo's eyes as I said it. But I wasn't willing to divulge the full truth. Not yet, at least.

"That's awfully altruistic of you." A faint smile had appeared. "But that's not why scientists mapped the human genome. And forgive my forwardness, but an encantado doesn't come all the way from Brazil to the frigid north to conduct her research at McGill just out of curiosity."

My eyes darted to hers. A clear-eyed one, this Serena Russo—probably in more ways than one.

"If you don't mind, I'd like to hear the real reason," she said, blue eyes close on me. "Why are you studying the DNA of your fellow Others?"

I discovered my lips moving—words coming out of them—before I'd even fully processed her question. "Because we're dying out," I breathed.

GoneGodDamn, I hadn't meant to say that, but something about her compelled me to share my true motives.

One of her coal eyebrows went up. "Ah, so you know. Well, the 'Other Anti-Extinction Initiative' isn't exactly off the nose, is it?"

"We need to cure Other cancers." The words spilled out of me now. "And alzheimers, and multiple sclerosis, and Parkinson's." That was the hard truth of my research: now that we were mortal, Others had become vulnerable. As members of our species now aged and died, we would slowly go extinct.

All of us.

"And of course," I said, nearly out of breath, "we need to be able to procreate."

There it was. My truth. I—and every other Other alive—couldn't have babies. We couldn't perpetuate our species, and as soon as the last of us died of old age, we would all be gone.

After the gods left, it was this knowledge that had led me to study at McGill. Because more than anything else, my mortal life's desire was to have a child. To know the possibility of motherhood.

But to do that, I first needed to map the triple helix.

Dr. Russo was nodding at me; her smile had grown, her eyes lit. "There it is. That's why we funded your work, Isabella. It's that passion you feel that earned you a grant for your research, and it's why I want you here Monday through Friday, four to nine. Can you do that?"

Five days a week, five hours a day? I ran through my schedule in my mind—eighteen credit hours of classes, eating, sleeping, Aimee, Justin (wait, was I already including Justin in my schedule? What did that mean?)—but my thoughts were cut short.

"Isa." Professor Allman set a hand on my arm. "This is an amazing opportunity."

I nodded, pushing everything else from my head. This was a huge grant and undertaking that would likely take a whole semester to implement, so I'd be able to scale down my classes anyway. "When do we start?"

Dr. Russo's eyes flitted from Professor Allman to me. "Tomorrow."

Nobody blinked. Nobody laughed. So I did, a little giggle. Then I realized she was dead serious. "Oh." I tapped my knuckles on the edge of the workstation with an echo. "OK. Tomorrow."

She smiled, and despite getting everything I'd wanted (and so much more), the blackness tugging at my mind didn't dissipate at all.

CHAPTER SIXTEEN

*T*he next day, I shut his office door and dropped into Professor Allman's armchair. He was still going on about the research grant and the work I would be doing with Dr. Russo, but I had dragged him back here as soon as we could politely get away.

The truth was, I just wanted to talk about the murders. I felt somehow responsible for figuring out what had happened to the two students who had been killed. Maybe it was because I couldn't get that agonized face out of my mind, or maybe it was because, ever since I'd taken on the illusion of Katrina Darling, a little bit of her had seeped into me.

Whatever it was, I knew the stymphalian birds were intrinsically connected to it all. And no one had a better mind than Professor Allman. Especially for creatures of lore.

I reached into my purse. "You have to promise me you won't freak out when I show you this."

He set his reading glasses on, sitting across from me. "You say it's a bird's feather? I can't imagine why I would ... Oh."

When he saw what I'd pulled out, he went silent. I extended the bronze feather toward him, and he received it with two hands. "You say these were all over the street last night?"

"My boyfriend—I mean, friend—pulled this one out of a car. It went right into the metal."

His eyebrows went up over the rims of his glasses. "And the rest?"

"They went everywhere—through windows, into the sides of buildings, even into the ground—except people. They didn't hit anyone."

He turned the feather from end to end, tipped it onto its side. "Curious."

"That's right. Professor, I did some research this morning—they're stymphalian birds from Greek mythology."

He nodded. "Oh yes, I suspected that right away. I can't think of another bird species of lore described this way."

"The part I can't explain," I said, "is why they didn't actually kill anyone last night. But I'm sure you heard about the two murders."

Now his eyebrows lowered, a gloom settling over his features. "Two students. One off-campus, and one right here outside his dorm. An awful thing."

"I know—I was the first person to see the victim on Saint Catherine Street." I took a deep breath. "His heart had been taken from his chest. It was almost like someone had reached in and scooped it out."

Professor Allman eyed me. "Isabella, do you think it was the birds?"

"No," I said. "I saw them attack. The birds didn't actually hurt anyone—it was all a distraction. And you can see that wing for yourself ... If they'd wanted to, they could have killed everyone on Saint Catherine."

"Oh yes," he said with more fervor than I liked. "The stymphalian birds were a terrible scourge in Greek mythology. They're uniquely lethal."

"I saw a flock of them in one of the trees outside my dorm this morning."

"And what did they do?"

"They just ... stared at me. And then they flew off."

He nodded slowly. "That makes sense. They're nocturnal killers—poor daytime vision."

I leaned forward. "I didn't see anything about that in my reading."

"Think about it. Where did these birds originate?"

I thought back to my reading. "It was ... the Stymphalian swamp." Apollo was said to detest the place. And if Apollo—the god of sun—wouldn't go there, then the swamp must have been a place where the sun literally didn't shine.

If that was true, then it would make sense that they were nocturnal hunters.

His hands went out expectantly.

"They prefer a lack of light," I said slowly. "They're nocturnal, as you say."

He lifted the feather closer to his face, holding it before him like a blade, inspecting the edges and flat of it with reverence. "Remarkable."

I took a deep breath. "What if they were commanded by someone else? The real killer."

He glanced up from his close inspection. "How do you reckon?"

"The killings are too alike in profile. It was nighttime. One victim ended up missing a heart, the other his eyes. And they're both young men. Professor, were there any creatures in Greek mythology who preyed on young men?"

His eyes drifted, thumb touching the scruff at his chin. He'd always done this when something captivated him, and I felt a surge of excitement that his mind was fully set on this mystery. "Yes," he said finally. "More than one. But my knowledge of the Greeks isn't so extensive as with South American creatures of lore. Have you researched it?"

"I just came up with this theory on my way over. I've only researched the birds."

"I think you're onto something, Isa." He stood, paced two feet left, came to stand with his hands on the back of the armchair. "And if what you're thinking is actually the case, that won't bode well for Others."

That hadn't occurred to me, but he was right: if it was an Other perpetrating these murders—and it almost certainly was—whenever this individual was caught, it would reflect badly on all Others.

And that was the last thing we needed right now. For some reason, when it came to human violence, humans were able to distinguish between awful members of their species and the rest. But not Others —when one of us ran amok, we all got the shaft.

"So if I go to the local police, they'll probably be on the lookout for an Other," I said. And given how little information they probably had about the suspect, that could quickly devolve into a witch hunt.

"If you go to them," he said, "I advise you to do your research beforehand. Be very specific about the Other you think is responsible for these killings."

I nodded. We were clearly on the same page.

When I stood, he escorted me to the door. "Isabella," he said before I left. I turned toward him, and he passed me the bronze feather. "Be careful. Don't stay out alone at night."

"I won't." Though if my theory was correct, it wasn't me who needed to worry about being out alone at night.

Justin, I thought with a squeeze of the heart.

↔

I arrived at the O³ house at mid-afternoon. No one answered until the third round of knocking, and then it was a Miss Doubtfire-esque woman with a feather duster staring back at me. "Yes?"

They employ a maid service? Really? There were some things I had to get over about Justin's frat life, but this wasn't one of them.

"Hello ma'am. May I come in to see Justin Truly?"

She shook her head. "All out."

"They're all out? Where?"

"Gym. McGill gym."

She must have meant the rec center on campus. I raised a hand, thanking her before I turned away to make my way back onto campus and to where the whole O³ house was apparently doing a group workout.

Which, probably to their horror, struck me as deeply erotic. Twenty sweaty young men, grunting and flexing together? I mean, everything about fraternal tradition suggested as much, which made their absolute obsession with women a little hilarious to me.

But, I thought as I arrived at the gym and pulled open the massive doors, *I wouldn't even mind if Justin swung both ways.* After all, few people were 100% straight, and as a distinctly sexual Other, who was I to stand in the way of someone's desires?

Except all my illusions about a group workout were destroyed when I stepped inside and saw the big stand-up poster greeting me. *WORLD ARMY CADET TRAINING,* it read. *TODAY AT 2PM IN ROOM 113.*

Beneath the lettering sat the World Army's logo, and I nearly gagged. I knew Justin had gotten involved, but was the whole O^3 house in on this now? And how often were they participating in these trainings? I'd thought they'd meet up maybe once a week, but as I came to Room 113 and looked in through the door, I saw all twenty of them engaged in a very particular form of self-defense training.

I'd taken self-defense training before. It involved striking the most vulnerable points on a person's body—a human's body: the eyes, the groin, the neck. But they weren't going for the typical places. In fact, they weren't even fighting humans. Someone had drawn the short straw and now labored around the room in a three-headed dog costume, pretending to lunge at a few of them. In return, they swung at it with wooden practice swords.

It was self-defense against Others.

↔

I stared through the window, my mouth open. At the head of the group, whistle in hand, stood a man you could have pegged for a drill sergeant. Tall, blocky, shaved head and a muscle tee. He set the whistle between his lips, and a shrill noise filled the room. All motion ceased, and the twenty O³ frat boys—Justin among them—straightened, turned toward him.

The World Army's local cadet trainer.

And it was in turning toward him that Justin spotted me through the door. His face registered surprise before he swung away. One by one, the trainer passed down the line of them, retrieving their training swords. He directed them to a wall fitted with a series of bows and quivers of arrows.

"Minatours have blind spots, just like bulls," he explained. "Try to stay directly in front of them and you just might have an edge. As for a cyclops, there's only one target you should aim for: their eye. And when fighting a wendigo, go for behind the knees. That'll send them tumbling."

"What about a dragon?" one of the cadets asked.

"A dragon, son? Well, if you're up against one of those, there's only one effective strategy that I know of … run."

Laughter echoed through the room.

That was when I spun away and walked over to the nearest bench. It was where I was still seated when Justin and the other cadets walked out of the training room.

At the back of the group walked Justin and the trainer. They stood by the door, and the World Army man clapped Justin on the shoulder. He grinned back. I didn't hear everything, but I did make out, "Good job, son," before the man turned away and proceeded down the hall in that smug, militaristic style.

Justin, his grin still wide, came over to me, hands finding his jeans' pockets. "Hey, Isa. I didn't think you'd—"

"You didn't think I'd come here." I knew exactly what he would say, because it was what every vaguely ashamed lover says. As an encantado, I knew how the back-and-forth went better than anyone. And right now, I didn't have the patience to let the whole script play out.

He shrugged, nodded. "I'm glad you're here, though."

I turned my face up to meet his eyes. "Oh?"

"I saw you peeking in through the window. Pretty cool stuff, huh?"

"Which part—slapping a guy in a cerberus costume with your wooden sword, or the brainwashing?"

To his credit, he didn't say anything. If he had—even one word—I might have launched into a rant in Portuguese. When he sat down next to me and took my hand, I felt myself easing toward him against my own will. He stroked my fingers.

"Why are you a part of that?" I whispered. "It's a hateful group."

"We're learning to defend ourselves."

"What about self-defense against other humans? Why a cerberus?"

"Come on, Isa. You know that whoever committed those two murders wasn't human. There's an Other running around campus killing people, and I want to be ready."

Well, he was right about the murdering Other, which pissed me off even more. Because even though I had come here to tell him to take care of himself and explain everything I suspected about these crimes, everything I said would only add to his burgeoning beliefs. I would just confirm his feelings about Others.

Others were the "other."

I stared down at our touching hands and sighed. Whatever his feelings, I still knew my own feelings for him. "I came here to warn you. I did some research, and I believe whoever is doing these killings is targeting young men—specifically at night."

"An Other," he said. "Like Sergeant Johnson thought. Do you have any ideas about the species?"

His name is really Sergeant Johnson? If everything about a man ever screamed rah-rah-xenophobic-nationalism, it was that World Army recruiter. And his name suited him to a tee, but I didn't think Justin would appreciate me saying so.

"I'm not sure yet," I said, "but I think it's a creature from Greek mythology. I discovered today that those birds are called stymphalian birds, and I believe they could be controlled by someone."

"You said Greek mythology?"

I nodded.

"Isa, you're brilliant." I glanced up into a pair of blue, lit eyes. His mouth was so close I could feel his breath. "We need to go." He stood, pulling me up.

"Where?"

"Well, we're not going to narrow down the candidates for murdering Other from Greek mythology in the weight room, are we?"

And as much as I wanted to object, to be mad, something melted in me as he led me down the hallway, my hand clasped in his. Thoughts of being taken and ravaged by his strong hands flowed into my head as we walked, and all my frustrations with him were shoved to the attic of my mind.

He glanced back at me. "You want to save a young man's life, don't you?"

And all I could do was nod. Well, there you have it—the encantado weakness. GoneGoddess Yemoja help me.

CHAPTER SEVENTEEN

Twenty minutes later, we stood outside the Pointe-a-Calliere Museum. Was this another attempt to show me how cultured and liberal artsy he was? A few days ago he'd taken me to a local art exhibit, where he'd spent the whole time with his fingers on his chin.

I turned to him. "Justin, I don't think …"

He held a finger to his lips. "Just trust me."

Trust him. Well, after everything we'd been through with El Lobizon, nearly drowning and a decades-old grudge that had nearly resulted in catastrophe, I could do that. Easily. So we walked into the museum and he paid for our tickets.

Five minutes later, we stood at the entrance to an exhibit on Greek mythology. Before us sat artifacts and old books laid open and every creature from Greek legend and lore documented on the walls.

Or at least, that was what the placard claimed.

"How?" I whispered, stepping up to the display on Artemis. Before me sat an intricate series of pots and plates painted with depictions of the huntress. Along with a detailed description of her importance to the Greek pantheon. "How did you know this was going on right now?"

"Believe it or not, I did some research of my own."

I glanced up at him. "What do you mean?"

"I had the same suspicions as you about the birds, and I did some Googling based on their characteristics. But I hadn't made the connection to an Other from Greek lore controlling them."

I grinned at him. "And here I thought of you as a frat bro."

He set one hand to his chest. "Isabella, dost thou stereotype? I am a human unlike all other humans."

"Touche." I turned away. His point was well taken: mentally, I had lumped him in with all of Greek life. Just like I was accusing him of doing to Others.

We walked through the exhibit, examining every god and creature and ruling them out one by one. We passed by Scylla the sea monster. "It can't have been something too big or crazy—people would have noticed on Saint Catherine," I said. "It probably looked human."

"What about this one?" He pointed to a creature known as Lamia.

I stepped close, inspecting her placard. She seemed a likely candidate, but … I shook my head. "No—she only killed children as revenge for Zeus killing her own."

Justin's fingers slid over mine as we moved on to the next placard, and he slowed us to a stop. "How have you been feeling—you know, since everything happened last night?"

I lowered my face. I hadn't taken much time to process anything that had happened in the last day. Did I even know how I was feeling? *Bad*, I thought as I listened to my gut. I felt really, really bad. Just a swirl of icky, black badness.

"Not good," I said. "It's been a long time since I've seen a dead man."

"Really? What about your lovers? I thought you had all sorts of men you loved."

I sighed. Was I about to deliver an important life lesson? "Love and lust rarely align for long," I said. "And men usually couldn't get past the mermaid-dolphin thing, which meant we didn't often grow old together."

"You said it had been a long time, but not never."

The last time I'd seen a man die was when Marco left the world, but I didn't know if I wanted to go there. I had only just recently been able to study birds again with the same joy I'd used to feel.

He led me toward one of the low couches in the middle of the exhibit, and we sat on it. Around us spread the entirety of Greek lore and legend. "Do you want to talk about it?" he asked.

Did I want to talk about it? Not really. Right now, I felt a strong compulsion to scour this entire exhibit until we came across the "aha!" creature. The one we could peg as the murderer. It was a scientist thing; we got no greater thrill than from a solvable mystery, one with a definitive answer.

And then I remembered that I was expected to start working for Dr. Russo tomorrow … and on into the indefinite future.

"Justin," I said, "there's something else we need to talk about. Remember that grant I mentioned?"

He nodded. "To support your research on Others."

"Well, this woman who's my new lead, Dr. Russo, is expecting me to spend basically all my free time—"

He held up a hand. "Did you say Russo? As in, Serena Russo?"

"Yes …?"

Justin looked like he'd just seen a celebrity. "You met her?"

"In the olive-skinned flesh. Why—what's up?"

"Sergeant Johnson mentioned she was on campus, but I never even thought I'd get a glimpse of her. And you're going to be working under her! Wait until I tell the O^3 guys."

I set my hands on Justin's shoulders. "Hold up. What are you talking about? You don't give a flip about biology."

He looked wounded. "In the sense that I am a biological creature, I very much do."

"Fine. But how do you know about Dr. Russo?"

"She's one of the World Army's top scientists." A small grin spread across his face. "Leading the way toward a brighter future."

Oh boy. It seemed the koolaid was plentiful, and Justin was drunk on it. And then his words fully processed: the World Army's top scientist. I shrank away, staring at my own fingers in my lap.

"What is it, Isa?"

The buzzing in my ears drowned him out. I was working for Dr. Russo. By extension, I was working for the World Army. Why was the World Army investing in Other anti-extinction research? Didn't they want to see every Other wiped off the Earth?

I squeezed my eyes shut. Now I had two puzzles in my head, and as much as I wanted to focus on where we were right now, my brain would never stop trying to navigate both until I had gotten through one and then the other.

Maybe I should quit my research at the lab. The last thing I wanted was to be a pawn of the World Army. But then again, they were doing important work, and Dr. Russo hadn't just "made it rain," as they say —she'd brought a thunderstorm of dollar bills and planted it right over my head.

My timeline for mapping the triple helix was about to get much, much shorter. Maybe if I just hung on for a while ...

Justin was trying to get my attention. His hand was on my shoulder now, shaking it.

"What is it?" I snapped, flaring on him.

He pointed at the far wall. "That."

My gaze followed, and my anger died. All my attention zeroed in on the image on the far wall, and the two of us stood together and crossed over to it. We stood in silence as we read the placard.

"*Merda*," I whispered after I'd finished reading. "That's the murderer."

↔

Empusa. She was the daughter of the goddess Hecate and the spirit Mormo, and she feasted on young men. She was a shapeshifter who played on your fears, often taking the form of that which frightened you the most. Notably, she always appeared to be missing a body part.

Heart. Eyes. Was she harvesting these boys' parts?

As I stood in front of the exhibit, I understood why I hadn't heard of her; she was only mentioned in a few pieces of literature: two of Aristophanes' plays and a biography, *Life of Apollonius of Tyana*.

"But both of those men were killed at night," Justin said. "It doesn't say anything here about her being a nocturnal huntress."

I set a finger to the placard. "She attacks young men *while they sleep*. Nocturnal. The one they found in a tree on campus ... that tree was right next to his dorm."

"The one we found that night hadn't been sleeping, though."

I glanced up at Justin. "Are you sure about that?"

"What do you mean?"

"There are apartments above some of the buildings on Saint Catherine Street, aren't there?" I turned away from the display. "And think about the way he was slumped against the wall. Remember how his leg was bent under him?"

"You think he fell from a window?"

"Or he was thrown."

He nodded. "She's probably not done, either. She's still out there."

I thought back to Professor Allman's advice about not talking to the cops until I had a specific suspect in mind. Well, now we did. "We should go to the police. Let them know our suspicions."

He nodded. "And I'm going to see Sergeant Johnson. I think the World Army would be very interested to know such a dangerous Other is wandering around the city, picking off students."

I made a face.

"What?" he said.

"It's just ... getting the World Army involved is worse than the police. They're not very Other-friendly."

"Uh, in case you hadn't noticed, Isa, this Other isn't very human-friendly. And as soldiers, we're training to deal with situations like this."

My eyes widened on him. "You're a soldier now?"

I could tell he hadn't wanted to deliver the news to me this way, here in the museum. But a certain pride burned in his eyes as he stared back at me. "I am." He paused. "At least, I want to be. Need to be."

"Why?" I said, though I suspected I knew.

He sighed, lowered his face. "This is embarrassing to talk about."

I set a hand on his leg. "What is?"

He mumbled something too quietly for me to understand, but it sounded like ...

"You were possessed by a demon?" I repeated, leaning closer.

His head seemed to hang lower. "That's right."

"How?"

And he explained the whole story: dybbuk's box and speaking when he shouldn't have—"so stupid of me," he said—and ending up with the demon inside him. How he'd tried to kill everyone he knew. In the end, Katrina had saved the day.

"Just like she always did," he ended. "Once again, my girlfriend saved me."

"It's OK," I said. "It's—"

He raised his face, that flame now returned to his eyes. "I'm different now. I'm not weak like that anymore."

"You weren't weak, Justin. You're only human."

"*Only* human. It's a shame being only human, isn't it?"

I blinked, shook my head. "No."

This was shaping up to be our first fight, and even as I felt ashamed and embarrassed and wanted to end it, I also felt a certain anger flaring in me. Anger at his anger. Frustration at his choice to become a soldier for the World Army.

It must have shown on my face, because he reached into his pocket and pulled out a coin. He held it out to me. "Can you flick this off your thumb? Straight up?"

I took it. "Of course I can."

"Good. Do it." He closed his eyes and waited.

"What's the point of this?"

His eyes remained shut. "Just do it."

So I set the coin on my thumb and launched it into the air. As it reached the height of its arc, Justin's hand flicked up and the fingers closed around it. He lowered his closed hand, extending it between us. When his palm opened—the coin at the center—so did his eyes.

I swallowed. I knew he had good reflexes, but pulling a coin out of the air with his eyes closed? "How did you do that?" I whispered.

"I'm not weak anymore," he repeated.

"What does that mean?"

He pushed the coin back into his pocket. "It means I'm being trained to handle myself. I've been pushing myself to learn all sorts of new things."

Justin couldn't have been a cadet for more than a couple weeks, and as a biologist, I knew as well as anyone that muscle memory took time. More time than he'd had. But I kept my thoughts to myself; Justin looked so happy.

Still, this made me uneasy.

"Wonderful," I said. The word lingered in the air, and I felt it again: that wedge between us. It had grown. "Well, I can cover the police front, and you can handle the World Army front."

He glanced back up at me. "You don't want me to come with you to the station?"

"I..."

The truth was, I did want him to come with me. I'd felt completely uncomfortable around Tremblay, and having Justin there as my human ambassador would probably help to grease the groove. At the same time, I hated thinking I needed an *ambassador* just to talk to the police. Principle and my own pride made me want to go it alone.

We stared at each other for a while, and my gaze finally drifted to the image of Empusa behind him. She might be out there still, somewhere on the campus. I shivered, crossing over to Justin and setting my hand on his forearm. As soon as we touched, that iciness dissipated. "Until this is resolved," I said, "I don't want to let you out of my sight."

He smiled at me. "Does this mean I get to sleep on the floor of your dorm?"

I blinked. "Actually, that's a good idea."

His smile grew, and a name popped into my head.

His girlfriend's name. I remembered for the hundredth time: *Justin's with Kat. Justin's with Kat.*

I sighed. "Have you talked to Kat yet?"

"Not yet." A cloud passed over his face. "She's been ... incommunicado."

He and I may have already slept together twice, but that was when he thought I was Katrina. Not when he knew I was me. Things were different now. And before we got together—truly together—I wanted him to make things right with Katrina. It was the only way any of this had a hope of longevity. And I wanted longevity.

I forced a neutral expression before I looked up at him. "Talk to her," I said. "OK?"

"I will," he said with utter seriousness. Then that spark returned. "But I still get to sleep on your floor tonight."

I nodded slowly. "For your protection."

"Right. Maybe I should wear one of your nightgowns, too."

I glared. "It won't fit."

"Empusa won't suspect me in a floral nightgown."

We pushed the museum doors open, stepped into the daylight. "You're way too irreverent about this whole situation."

"One thing I learned from Kat," he said, a certain wistfulness entering his voice, "irreverence can be a great weapon against your enemies."

CHAPTER EIGHTEEN

$\mathcal{W}$e came into the police station and walked up to the desk, where a forty-something female officer sat with forms strewn in front of her. As we waited to be acknowledged, she scratched at her brown bun with one finger and didn't lift her eyes from the paper she was filling in.

Her pen just kept scratching.

It occurred to me that the police station used to have a valkyrie officer roaming campus, or maybe I was imagining things. Maybe the valkyrie had just been a student, and I just hoped the police force employed an Other. Because right now, they were looking pretty universally human.

"Hi there," Justin finally said.

Her eyes lifted, wanton and tired. When they settled on Justin, a tiny flame burst into life. "How can I help you?"

I sighed; the halo effect.

Before Justin could answer, I stepped forward. "We're here about the two murdered McGill students. We believe we know who the suspect is."

Her eyes trailed reluctantly over to me. "Who are you two?"

"We're students at McGill." She looked unimpressed, so I added,

"We were the first two on the scene of the murder on Saint Catherine Street. I spoke with Officer Tremblay last night."

Her eyebrows went up. Apparently I had strung all the right words together. "All right." She lifted her pen, pointed at a row of chairs. "I'll see if I can get you in to talk to him."

We sat, and she went back to her forms. Around us, the only noises were the sounds of her pen and a wall clock ticking down the time until evening came again.

Evening, and *her*. The killer, Empusa.

Justin leaned toward me, eyes on the officer. "I'll bet this is the last thing she expected when she signed up for the force."

"Who knows." This woman worked in a warm, relatively non-stressful environment compared to most officers on duty. "Maybe this was exactly what she expected."

I glanced over at Justin, who sat ramrod straight in his chair. His left leg had fallen into a slight jiggle, and I knew what he meant was: this was the last thing he expected for *himself*. He'd rather be out there, in the world, climbing mountains and fighting three-headed dogs. He was all physicality and action and utilizing each of his senses.

But I could sense this was new. He wasn't always like this. Justin, with all his gung-ho-ness, was a man with something to prove. But unlike so many men who set goals to prove their worth to themselves, I got the sense that Justin needed to prove his worthiness to someone else.

That someone: Kat.

I've seen love drive men to acts of insanity for love. Justin loved Kat. *Loves* Kat.

I just hoped he had the good sense to navigate those mountains and three-headed dogs—and people like Sergeant Johnson and the World Army—without getting himself killed. I worried about him; I could at least burn time to use magic, but he was just ... human. All he had were his (ample) brawn and his brains.

And, of course, his halo effect.

Ten minutes later, a door opened. Officer Tremblay appeared, his eyes settling on Justin at once. He gestured us into his office, where we sat down opposite him at his desk.

Before he could ask any questions, I launched right into it. "Officer," I said, "we've been doing research, and we think we know who was behind those two murders. And she's very likely not done terrorizing the city."

To his credit, Tremblay jumped right into it with me. "She?"

"An Other from Greek mythology called Empusa," I said. "She's a shapeshifter who preys on young men."

"A shapeshifter."

"Right."

"An Other from Greek mythology."

"Right." How many times was I going to have to confirm what I'd just said? "She always appears missing a body part—a leg or eyes or an arm. And she especially craves young men for the freshness and purity of their—"

He exhaled. "I still can't get my head around this kind of talk. A few years ago, the worst criminals were druggies and drunk college kids."

"It's not talk—it's a solid lead," I said, irritation rising in me. "She's actually out there, and she's going to kill another male student. It's in her nature, and McGill is like Candy Land."

Tremblay looked surprised, sitting back in his chair. "OK," he said, arms folding over his chest. "So you're telling us to be on the lookout tonight for this Empusa." Once again, I could tell he wasn't sold on whatever I had to say. He knew I was an encantado—an Other.

I kept trying. "You should alert the campus administration so they can take steps to protect the male students."

The tiniest smile bloomed on Tremblay's face, so small I could have mistaken it simply for interest in what I was saying. "Like lock them all up in a gymnasium with coffee to keep them awake?"

I wanted to sock him in his vaguely amused mouth. "That would be at least doing something."

His eyes drifted to Justin. "You said you're one of those World Army cadets."

"Yes, sir."

"Has Sergeant Johnson been made aware of this Empusa ahead of tonight's patrol?"

I looked over at Justin. "Patrol?"

"Not yet, sir. I was planning to tell him this evening." He glanced over at me, apology written on his face, before returning his attention to Tremblay. "If Empusa is the Other responsible—and I believe she is —we'll be safer on patrol than asleep."

"We?" I said. "I thought you were going to be sleeping in my dorm tonight. Wearing my nightgown."

Tremblay's eyebrows went up again, and Justin's cheeks reddened. "I was just joking around with you, Isa." He turned fully toward me now, taking one of my hands in his. "I'd already volunteered to be part of the squad patrolling campus after sundown. We'll be going half the night."

My mouth hung open. They hadn't even known about Empusa when Justin volunteered, which meant this World Army patrol around campus had been in the works.

"This sounds a lot like security theater," I blurted. "A lot like a bunch of students with false, martial authority." The worst part: Justin had been planning to do this all day, and he hadn't bothered to tell me.

Justin dropped my hand. "We're protecting this campus."

"Well," Tremblay said, "if you see anything, do not engage. Call us —the number's on the wall." He pointed at a sign with 911 written on it. "We've got a whole slew of equipment for dealing with Others of just about every species ..."

I stood, set my fingers on the desk. I wasn't about to listen to him detail all his anti-Other gear. And I was getting angrier and angrier that Justin had hid this patrol from me. "Well, Officer, I've told you everything I came to tell you. Thank you for your time."

Before Tremblay or Justin could react, I grabbed my purse and walked out of his office. When the door closed behind me, the female officer didn't glance up from her paperwork. And even though I hoped—expected, even—Justin would come after me, he didn't.

No one did.

↔

The next morning, I woke to another murder.

At some point Aimee had crawled into bed with me—which was unusual, given she usually woke up way, way earlier than me—and was spooning me like a baby koala on its mother's back. When I sat up, she murmured, "Don't go. It's too scary out there."

"What are you talking about?"

"I went to the dining hall for breakfast, and everyone was crying. It's so sad."

I turned toward her, pushing my hair out of my face. "What's sad?"

Not Justin, I selfishly thought. *Whatever happened, please don't let it be Justin.* Because if something had happened to him, it would have been because I had just walked out of the police station and left him alone. Even when I knew what he was going to do, and what Empusa was all about.

Aimee's eyes finally opened, and she pulled the covers tight around her. "The student body president was discovered dead in his bed. Missing his tongue."

"His tongue?" I repeated, my insides turning over. My stomach was empty, but I felt nauseous.

She nodded. "There's going to be a curfew from now on. No students out after dark until they find the killer."

After dark. So Tremblay had probably followed my lead about Empusa being a nocturnal killer. Or they were just going by the data: three deaths, all at night.

And then there was the fact of the curfew. Because of these deaths, our entire lives were being affected. This school was becoming a frightened, frightening place. Which I knew would only get worse the longer the killings went on.

"The worst part," Aimee said, "were the stories of those birds. Apparently they swarmed on campus last night, diving people and attacking them. Everyone was terrified, and a few people even got hurt."

"When?"

"When what?"

"When did the birds attack? Was it the same time as the murder?"

She shrugged beneath the comforter. "I don't know, Isa."

Almost certainly they'd happened at the same time. I climbed out of bed, fully awake now. When I glanced at the clock—GoneGod-Damn, I was late for work at the lab—I started my familiar rush around the room, dressing and brushing my teeth all at once.

Then I remembered today was my first day working under Dr. Russo, the World Army's top scientist. The same World Army who was currently turning my sort-of boyfriend from a student into a soldier.

Dr. Russo had respect. She had sway. And she was a top researcher of Other DNA … which meant I could take my lead about Empusa straight to the top and maybe be taken seriously. She might even have ideas for how to capture this Other and end the murders.

I swallowed as I left the dorm and started walking to the biology building. The World Army. It seemed like they were closing in on my life from every front. Justin. My research. Campus patrol.

Be brave, Isa, I repeated to myself as I came into the building and walked down the hallway past the research labs where I had spent all my time working, and where Dr. Russo's Other Anti-Extinction project was now taking place.

As in, literally *right now.*

I stopped short as I passed one of the doors, glanced left through the small window into the lab room. A sign had been posted since yesterday: OTHER ANTI-EXTINCTION INITIATIVE PERSONNEL ONLY.

Personnel. That word belonged exclusively to stick-up-their-ass organizations like the World Army.

When I came to the door, it was still a knob-turn, but they had begun to install what looked like a keycard entry for extra security. Would I be required to use a keycard to get into the lab from now on? And since when did research in the biology department of a university require this kind of security?

I stood on my toes to see through the small window. Inside, I caught a glimpse of Dr. Russo's waterfall of black hair as she turned and came toward the door. Here was the woman I wanted to talk to about Empusa, and yet another impulse surged in me.

She was coming, and the two impulses battled for a half-second before the newer, dumb one won out. I jerked back from the window, falling against the wall just before the door opened, casting me in its shadow as she came tap-tapping out in her high heels and white jacket, her purse slung over her shoulder. She walked right on past in a hurry and never even noticed me.

I glanced at my phone in my bag. Right, it was the lunch hour.

Before the door could shut, I caught the knob. Even though I was 100%, completely allowed in this lab—my workstation was in here, after all—I felt like I was doing something illicit. Was I even "Other Anti-Extinction Initiative personnel?" Not yet, but I would be. I was part of their grant, one of their key researchers.

Which was why I stepped inside the lab and started looking around. Standard procedure on the first day on the job, right? Every employee has to get the lay of the land. And what I discovered was a completely different laboratory than the one I'd spent my undergraduate life working in. This place was full of top-notch equipment, machines I didn't even know how to use. One of them was bigger than me and looked like a gigantic waffle iron.

Despite everything, I felt vaguely giddy. The biology department had always been seriously underfunded, and even though I wanted to drive a hot poker through the World Army's logo every time I saw it, visions of the advances I could make for Otherdom were dancing through my mind.

"Hello?" I called.

No answer.

So I was alone. For now.

New partitions had been installed, doors added. I peeked in through a couple of them and discovered more equipment, some of it still in its wrapping.

One door was locked, the keycard unit already fully functional. It didn't have a window, and the walls weren't partitions like the rest.

This was a solid room they'd installed, and it was the only one the World Army had completely secured.

The rules of any good psychological thriller dictated that the key to a nefarious organization's plans lay behind the ultra-secure door labeled with a gold-lettered placard reading: *Dr. Serena Russo, Head of OAEI.*

OAEI. Other Anti-Extinction Initiative.

I set my ear to her door and listened, though I didn't know what I expected to hear. Evil whispers? Of course, I heard nothing but the whistle of the heating vent above me.

I tried the knob anyway, just for kicks. And by the GoneGods, it opened right up.

New rule: always try the most obvious option first.

I pushed the door open, and as I passed through the threshold, the scent changed to something citrus and fragrant. It even smelled nicer in here, not to mention the array of right-out-of-the-box equipment arrayed around the room. Several microscopes of varying sizes, slides, petri dishes, dyes, forceps, two Bunsen burners.

And one particular microscope sitting prettily in the center of her desk with a petri dish in it.

I came around her desk to where Russo had evidently been hard at work before she left. At this point, I knew I was way, way out of bounds. Unequivocally. If Dr. Russo or Professor Allman had walked in right now, I would be toast, as Americans say.

But despite my fascination with science, I'd always trusted my gut. And right now, my gut was telling me that I should be breaking a few rules. Namely, I should be snooping into this World Army scientist's very important work.

Because I might not get another chance.

Before me stood the fanciest microscope I'd ever seen, much less set my face to. What can I say? I'd spotted a petri dish under the lens, and a magnified petri dish is an impossible-to-resist lure for any biologist.

I lowered my face to the eyepiece. And I saw something I'd never seen before.

An unfertilized Other embryo.

I knew right away it wasn't human, because I'd spent a great deal of time studying human embryos. And this looked nothing like a human embryo. It was twice the size, and instead of being round like a human's, it was oblong.

Dr. Russo was studying Other reproduction. Which meant the World Army was studying Other reproduction.

Oh my GoneGods. Or as we encantado liked to say in Brazil, *Goddess Yemoja!*

The thing was this: Others were completely barren. After the gods left and we became mortal, we had been given the reproductive parts, but they just didn't work. We had the eggs, the spermatozoa, but they were inert. They didn't make magic (well, in the fluid-exchanging, squishing our parts together, baby-making sense).

Except I had always known it was possible. Or maybe it was a reckless hope that had led me to study Other DNA. I knew that without the third strand of the helix mapped, all of it was for naught. Embryos couldn't be fertilized and babies couldn't be born.

Which was why I'd spent the past year and a half on that preliminary step, and only now was I getting anywhere with the mapping.

I stood up straight, my heart galloping. My hand went to my chest, slid down to my belly. My intentions had been pure—good. I just wanted Others to live on, to be able to procreate if they wished.

I wanted to be able to procreate. To have a baby.

But the World Army's intentions? Well, they were an army. No matter what they claimed, one prerogative would always take priority: protect humanity above all else. Which didn't mean anything good for these Other embryos, these future babies—if they ever managed to figure out how to make the egg and sperm come together.

Beside the microscope, a manila folder gently flapped under the heating vent like it was begging to be opened.

So I obliged.

Inside, I found a full profile of—as it turned out—one of the most powerful Others from antiquity. I flipped through images, details from lore and myth, and even relevant passages from the two plays and one biography in which she'd appeared.

The daughter of a goddess and a spirit.

Empusa.

Her unfertilized embryo sat in that petri dish.

CHAPTER NINETEEN

a s we say in Brazil, *isto vai dar molho.* Which literally translates to, "this is going to give sauce." And by sauce, we mean problems.

This was going to cause problems.

And I was a part of it.

Among three Museum escapees during Operation Three Dead Gods, I read in the folder. Questions flitted through my head, even as I kept scanning the pages. What museum? Why was the M capitalized? And since when were Others kept in *museums,* of all places?

A noise sounded—shoes tapping in the hallway. A very specific tap-tap. My eyes flitted up, and I shut the folder. I stepped away from the desk and practically flew out of Dr. Russo's room, pulling the door closed behind me. I had just reached the middle aisle between several workstations when the lab's main door creaked open and in she walked.

The exact person I didn't want to see.

"Ah, Isabella." Dr. Russo stopped sudden and set one hand over her chest. "I didn't expect anyone to be here."

Ditto. For whatever reason, she'd come back much faster than expected. And then I realized I was early. A few hours early, in fact. I tried to slow my breathing, to avoid looking like I'd just run out of the room not ten feet right of me—or like I'd seen something I unequivocally shouldn't have.

Empusa's embryo.

Stop thinking about Empusa's embryo. Think about anything else.

"I was excited to get started," I said.

She placed her jacket on the coat hanger, turned to survey me. I realized I still had my heavy jacket on from when I'd been outside. "I bet you are. Did you already take a spin around the new workspace? We've changed things up a bit in here."

I nodded, pulling off my coat and approaching to set it next to hers. "A bit. It really was a very large grant we received, wasn't it, Dr. Russo?"

She smiled down at me. I could hardly hold her gaze; those blue eyes were almost fluorescent. "Call me Serena. We believe this work is extremely important, and we've funded it accordingly."

She turned toward me, her eyes darting over my face. It made me feel awkward, and I averted my gaze as I turned away from the hanger. What was she looking for? Did she suspect?

"Sorry," she said. "I'm just always fascinated by Others. And I've never met an encantado before."

"Oh," I said. "Well, I guess that makes sense. There are only a few hundred of us, mostly in South America. And we like to pretend we're someone else when we're not swimming around in our natural form."

"That is what I hear ... I've read all about your species," Dr. Russo—Serena—chuckled. "I also read that you're quite powerful illusionists, and something vague about using amulets to store your magic."

A pang shot through me. My hand went by instinct to my neck, where my amulet used to be. Had always been, for the past four years —until last week. I still found myself reaching for it several times a day.

It had been my last illusion, my safeguard for when I grew ancient. I had given it to a woman who deserved it more than I did.

"Not store magic. Channel it actually. Yes," I said. "Some do."

If she noticed me reaching for my absent amulet, she didn't mention it. Instead, she said, "How does that work?"

My eyes lifted to her, and in that moment, I felt strongly that I should not tell her. Not just about the amulet, but about anything related to my kind. She was up to no good—if she had Empusa's embryo, that meant she'd had *very* close contact with Empusa—and no ally of mine.

At least, not until she proved unequivocally otherwise. And I doubted that would ever happen.

"I don't know." I kept my face as straight as possible. "What our amulets do has always been shrouded in mystery, except among the elders."

"And you're not an elder."

"No—at five hundred years old, I'm one of the last born."

"Don't you mean created? By your gods."

My heart saddened at the thought. It was true that even before the gods left, we were created rather than born. Something that Serena had just pointed out with clinical detachment. She was stating a fact.

A fact that stung like a slap.

"Yes," I murmured.

"And how does that happen? How were you created, exactly?"

I shook my head. "I don't know. That was another secret held by the elders." *Elders who are in hiding now,* I thought.

I didn't want to continue talking about my creation, but I also didn't want to annoy my new boss. So I made a show of shifting my eyes toward the door. "Do you know if Professor Allman is around? I was supposed to meet him here so we could go over my most recent findings."

That was a lie, but it worked.

"No." Disappointment flickered across her face, but it disappeared just as fast. I guess working for the World Army gave you a lot of practice at veiling your emotions. "I'm afraid not. But since I'm working closely with the professor, I'd be very interested in your findings."

Well, at least we'd gotten off the let's-dissect-Isabella's-entire-history path. I led her over to my workstation, and she pulled up a stool as I showed her my progress mapping the third strand. I pulled out a few slides, set them under the microscope.

"This segment here," I said, "is one of many I'm examining for magic. I'm not totally sure, but I think a specific segment of our DNA is what allows us to use our magic in exchange for time."

"Remarkable." She stared into the microscope. She lifted her face away, turned toward me. She started talking about the possibilities for preventing cancer and alzheimer's, and how soon those would be realistic goals.

As she talked, my mind processed the information I'd seen in the manila folder. I had an almost-eidetic memory from hundreds of years of practice, and I could picture each piece of paper behind my eyes.

I understood now that Empusa took body parts because, whenever she appeared, she was missing one. Not always the same part—maybe a leg, or sometimes an arm. She was like Buffalo Bill from *Silence of the Lambs*, except the genders were reversed.

The most important piece of paper had been the last one I'd glimpsed before Serena came in. It explained the process for neutralizing Empusa. Except I hadn't gotten a chance to read the meat of it before Serena had interrupted me.

I needed to get back into that folder.

Another thought occurred to me: the World Army had such an acute understanding of this Other that they knew exactly who she liked to kill, and how, and most importantly, how to stop her.

Which meant Serena almost certainly knew all these things.

She was aware of the murders.

I focused on her, and suddenly, all her black-haired, blue-eyed beauty seemed to shrink, to bleach out. It was the opposite of the halo effect; sometimes, in learning more about a person, their beauty diminished. They became themselves in your eyes, and that was what had happened with Serena Russo.

I could look at her and experience none of the glamour. Under the harsh lighting, the fine lines and imperfections in her face came clear.

Tiny, imperceptible things under ordinary circumstances. But given what I knew about her, they were almost all I could see.

"Have you heard about the murders?" I interrupted. She'd been talking about pneumonia, and seemed surprised by my forwardness.

Normally I wasn't forward—except when I sensed injustice. And not you-took-my-parking-spot injustice, but real wrongs. In those moments, I was able to overcome my insecurities, my sense that I talked not enough or too much, or that my unworthiness seeped through my skin for everyone to see.

Chalk it up to hundreds of years of superficial infatuations, which almost always ended badly. I fell in love, but men didn't tend to react well when they discovered I wasn't the beautiful human they'd thought they were getting.

Fear of discovery was almost second-nature to an encantado. After all, who could love us as we were? Humans were most likely to take a dolphin captive or kill it.

And maybe that was why I'd sunk myself into my research on Other DNA. And lately, into figuring out the real story behind these murders. It made me feel worthy, capable—distracted me from that fear.

"Of course." Serena shook her head. "Terrible tragedies, all."

"They still haven't brought in a suspect." I watched her closely. I knew I was treading on porous ground, but like I said: injustice. I couldn't stop myself.

"That's my understanding." Her foot had started to tap, but she stopped it. She was getting suspicious, and I needed to scale it back.

I balled my hands in my lap. "I'm just so scared, Doctor. Do you think it's an Other who's doing it?"

Again, the blue eyes leveled on me. "It's hard to say."

I squeezed my eyes shut. "I'm sorry to be getting us so off topic. It's just … I was attacked by a flock of birds on the night of the murder on Saint Catherine Street."

"You were on Saint Catherine Street?"

"With my boyfriend, on a date. We ran into a bookstore to avoid them."

"How did the birds behave?"

I opened my eyes. I was a master at reading people, and Serena Russo wasn't displaying an ounce of concern. No ... she was intrigued.

"They shot their feathers at us. Metallic ones. And they had massive beaks and talons that they swiped when they dove for us."

"Did they hurt you?"

I shook my head. "By some miracle. But they definitely weren't regular birds. Doctor, you study Others. Do you know what they could have been?"

She raised a finger. "Ah, you're thinking in the anthropological sense. You see, I study the microscopic makeup of Others. Now if you asked me about the composition of an Other's cells, I'd be your girl."

I eyed her. Between the two of us, I wasn't the only one playing a role. I was the innocent, scared student. And somehow, she'd morphed into the nerdy, shut-in scientist I knew she wasn't and had never been.

More deception.

"Ohh," I said, nodding with wide eyes. "My mistake."

"It's hard for me to say what kind of birds they were without observing them." She pulled on her glasses, turned toward the microscope. "That said, it sounds like a curfew was the right choice on the administration's part."

Of course, I thought. Then, *Wait. Why "of course?"* Why would Serena Russo approve of the curfew? As often happened in tense situations, my subconscious mind understood something my conscious mind didn't. I realized my heart had been sledgehammering against my chest ever since she'd walked back in.

I was terrified.

"Serena, I'm going to use the restroom," I said, pushing myself up. "I'll be back."

She murmured assent, her face still pressed into the microscope.

I booked it down the hall into the bathroom. Inside, I dropped onto a toilet, bowing over until my head was nearly touching my thighs. I breathed hard, fast. *You haven't been caught. She didn't know you were looking through her papers,* I repeated in my head. *She didn't know.*

I repeated it until my breathing calmed, and I could sit up straight.

Empusa's embryo. Serena Russo. The World Army. Something massive had converged on this campus—something bigger than one killer. If she was studying Empusa, then she was studying other Others. Who knew how many profiles they had?

A quavering, powerful part of me wanted to bolt out of the bathroom and back to my dorm and climb under my floral comforter with Aimee. This was the encantado part of me, the side that knew I could slip out of anything. I could take on another illusion, become someone else.

All I had to do was run.

But then I thought of Justin. I thought of the people who had died, the kid sitting in the alley with his heart carved out. I thought of those who would still die because of Empusa—because of Serena Russo and the World Army. I, Isabella Ramirez, was who they'd picked to conduct their Other research. I would be granted daily access to their facilities. I didn't fully understand what was going on yet, but I had been given the keys, and I only needed to set them into the door and open it.

If I didn't, more young men would die to Empusa. And I would be responsible, because I was one of the few people who had access to the knowledge of how to stop her.

I got up, walked to the sinks, and turned on the faucet. Except I didn't move; my reflection was staring judgmentally back at me. "Well, Isa," I whispered, "you know what you have to do."

I set my hands under the water, clapped my wet fingers over my eyes, and fixed my hair before I walked back down the hallway to the laboratory.

Sometimes being a responsible adult sucked.

CHAPTER TWENTY

The next morning, I sat down across from Justin in our favorite cafe. Which was funny, given it was the same coffeehouse where I'd once been attacked by a vengeful Brazilian woman and—long story—ended up flopping around on the bathroom floor in my natural form.

All of which is to say, we'd playfully nicknamed it the Dolphin Cafe.

"You look like hell," he said.

I set both hands around my mug, observing the frothy rosette on the surface. "Charming."

"I meant it with the utmost affection." I glimpsed a small smile as his hand reached out to touch my wrist.

I managed a little upturn of the lips. "If I hadn't taken it that way, you'd have coffee all over your face right now." I raised my eyes to observe him. "You don't look like you slept, either."

He shrugged. "I didn't. Well, not much."

"I take it you didn't capture Empusa on your patrol last night." I tried to keep the sarcasm out of my voice, but a little seeped in.

If he'd noticed, he ignored it. "No—but maybe we spooked her. No murders, right?"

"No murders."

What a strange thing to be grateful for.

I took a deep breath, lifting my mug to take a sip. I was preparing to launch into the real reason I'd asked him here: to help me get access to Serena Russo's workstation and "borrow" that file on Empusa.

Yesterday while I'd been working at the lab, a couple security guys had finished activating the keycard entry on Serena's office door and the outer lab door. I'd received a keycard of my own, but I couldn't just go walking into her office anymore.

So I needed to break in. And I needed help.

All of this was going to create some serious cognitive dissonance for the World Army cadet sitting in front of me.

But Justin spoke up first. "We did see those birds again. They were swarming up near that cross at Mont Royal."

I almost dropped my mug. Instead, it clattered onto the small saucer and only spilled a little. "Did you go there?"

He nodded. "They had dispersed by the time we arrived. We didn't find anything."

No murders, no bodies. But the stymphalian birds had swarmed. Why? I needed to go there, to study the area with the kind of attention I suspected the World Army cadets hadn't—and couldn't have—given in the middle of the night.

Justin kept going. "Even so, I really feel like I'm helping, Isa. I feel like a part of something."

I focused on him. For the first time since we'd arrived, his blue eyes had brightened. "What 'something?' "

"A cause. I'm protecting this campus, and the people I care about."

"A cause."

He nodded, sitting straighter, as though the spirit of Sergeant Johnson stood next to us. "I've been a little uncertain about what I want to do with my life for ... well, basically all of college. But I'm starting to see a future now."

Unease filled me. "What kind of future?"

"As a protector. A few months ago, Kat and I dealt with, to put it bluntly, a superhero infestation on campus.

"I remember." I had walked by a crater the size of an elephant on my way to class that afternoon.

"Right. Well, back then I told her how much I would have loved to have superhero powers. Being a cadet makes me feel like I have those powers. Even if I am just a human. Part of it is just being with the other guys—the camaraderie and the commitment boosting us all."

"Commitment to what?"

He paused. I knew he was reconsidering his first response to my question—figuring out a more delicate phrasing. "To protecting this campus. But also to protecting the world."

I didn't say anything. I knew the more I questioned him, the closer we would get to the truth of it. To the wedge that existed between us.

He was committed to protecting humans from Others.

I took another sip of my coffee, and in those few moments, I knew I couldn't ask Justin to help me with this. It wasn't just the cognitive dissonance of working for the World Army and undermining it all at the same time. It was that, in asking Justin to help me, I would be tainting the goodwill and sweet connection between us. I would be hurting us.

And no matter what, I didn't want to hurt us.

I lowered my mug, pushing Serena Russo to the back of my mind. I allowed the encantado in me to emerge, leaning closer toward him. "You mentioned Kat. Did you and she talk?"

That brightness slipped from his eyes. "Not yet. I did get a call from a strange number, though."

"And you think it was her calling from that strange number?"

"I don't get many calls from random numbers in the middle of the night. And there was a voicemail ... I briefly heard breathing before it cut off."

"Her breathing?"

I waited, but Justin didn't offer up anything else. I knew he didn't want to admit how many times he'd probably listened to that voice-mail, trying to decipher the breathing on the other end. It would be embarrassing.

So I only slipped my hand across the table and touched his fingers. "When will she be back?"

He responded to the touch, gripping my fingers in his warmth. His thumb slid over my hand in a reassuring way. "I don't know. Soon, I hope. She and I need to talk." He paused. "I think we're going to break up."

I nodded as he stared at my hand. I wanted to be with him, and I was about to say as much, but something stopped me. It wasn't just that it was still too early. It was also that wedge, the stickiness of the World Army. Right now, despite our connection, we wanted very different things.

Most of all, it was clear he wasn't over Kat—that, at the very least, he still had something to prove to her.

So I squeezed his hand. "Justin, I care about you."

"But," he said.

" 'But?' "

"That was the precursor to a 'but …' "

I laughed. "Very perceptive, frat bro."

"It's almost like socializing all the time makes me socially aware."

"Touche. Yes, there's a but." I inhaled, removing my hand. "But you and she need to work out what's going on between you before anything more happens between us."

He watched my fingers disappear beneath the table. "If I were a lesser frat bro, I would think you're calling me a serial monogamist."

I lifted both hands, palms out to him. "Hey, encantado here."

And with surprising grace, he nodded. "I understand. But I want you to know that I really like you, Isa. I mean well."

It was time to get real. Really, uncomfortably real. "I really like you, too. The thing is," I blurted, "I'm not human."

He watched me, waiting for me to go on.

"I'm an Other. You saw my natural form."

In my long life, every man who'd beheld my true form—what amounted to a pink dolphin—had reacted in one of two ways: fear or disgust. And because I liked Justin so much, I didn't know if I could handle rejection. Not from him. So I'd held back every time the topic came up.

Except now I was out of excuses.

"I saw you," Justin said.

"And?"

"And I don't care what you look like."

My gut cinched, emotion rising up through my chest and neck and into my face. I wanted to push those words away. They had to be lies; they couldn't possibly be the truth.

"Just know that I'm trying to do the right thing by you both," he whispered.

"OK," I said. When he handed me a napkin, I realized I'd been crying. "I believe you."

↔

"So what you're saying is, Justin Truly potentially breaking up with Katrina Darling is the least interesting part of today?"

From her perch on the end of her bed, Aimee looked skeptical.

My eyes drifted from the TV, which I'd been watching for three mind-numbing hours as I debated how to move forward. It was helping my nerves, even if cable TV had turned into nothing but commercials. "That's what I'm saying."

"All right, change my mind."

So I told her about Dr. Serena Russo. The World Army. The file on Empusa, and what I'd seen under the microscope.

Finally, I told her what I needed to do in order to see that file again.

And sweet, cornflower-haired, blue-eyed Aimee? She laughed.

My arms folded over my chest. "I'm not joking."

"Oh."

"So, did I change your mind about my day?"

Within a few seconds, Aimee looked like someone had told her her dog had just died. Her eyes filled with tears, and she lifted both hands, gesturing for a hug.

When I sat down next to her, she wrapped her arms around me. She really was the most touchy-feely person I knew, and in an encantado's life, that was saying a lot. But it did feel nice.

"That's so dangerous, Isa," she said.

"I know."

"I'll help you."

I turned on her. "You'll what?"

The pale-blue eyes lifted. "I said I'll help you."

"But you just said it's dangerous."

"Justin's with the World Army now. You can't get him to help you infiltrate the evil scientist's workstation. Who else can you trust?"

I swallowed. Even if she was joking, *"the evil scientist's workstation"* didn't inspire much confidence in Aimee as my second. But she was right: who else could I trust? I felt strangely alone, vulnerable. The forces at work weren't just powerful ... they were lethal.

"You're shivering," Aimee said.

I glanced down, found my hands trembling on my thighs. I hadn't realized I'd been shaking. "I think I know where to find Empusa."

"Where?"

I closed my eyes; I couldn't stop shivering. "Maybe ... I don't know. My brain's a muddle."

Telling Aimee everything—and especially thinking of going after Empusa—had brought out such a visceral reaction that my heart had started into a hard pounding against my chest. My whole nervous system felt on edge.

I was a runner, not a fighter. And yet here I was, trying to be the opposite.

She rolled across her bed, popped open the side table drawer. With a crinkle, out came a little baggie.

"No," I said.

"Hear me out. Are you actually going to let me help you get into Dr. Russo's workstation?"

"No."

"Are you going to let me go with you to find Empusa?"

"Absolutely not."

"Do you have any idea how you're going to tackle either of those things?"

I paused. Then, "No."

She shook the bag. "This is how I can help you."

"I don't know how that's going to help," I said, even as I reached for it. Did I mention how susceptible encantado are to mind-altering drugs? And I had decided to be a college student. *Que bonito!*

Twenty minutes later, I sat with the phone to my ear. In a moment of hazy brilliance, we had figured out exactly what we needed to do.

Cancel our cable TV subscription.

I mean, we were only getting like fifty mediocre channels, and half the time we weren't even watching actual shows—just commercials. It was a total, infuriating ripoff.

Across the room, Aimee stared at me with big, red eyes. Smoke drifted around us.

"What?" I said.

"How long have you been on hold?"

I glanced at the clock on my desk. "Eighteen minutes." Elevator muzak rang in my left ear, and I reached for the blunt. Aimee passed it over.

"Why are you still staring at me?" I said.

"I had a thought."

"About the whole World Army-Dr. Russo-Empusa situation?"

She shook her head.

"OK—what?"

"If you burned time to get you off hold faster, would you actually be saving time, or losing it?"

I blinked. My mouth opened, closed again. "No," I said. "Just no."

"One minute."

"That's one minute off my life, Aimee!"

"You've been alive since like, 1502."

"Hey, you swore you wouldn't talk about my age."

"Yeah, in public."

"I'm not burning time to get off hold faster."

"Thirty seconds."

I was about to disappoint her again, but something on the shelf by her head caught my eye. Professor Allman's textbook.

She followed my gaze. "Don't tell me you're thinking about biology."

"I'm thinking about biology," I said, setting the phone down. "Aimee, you're a genius."

"Well, yes …"

"Professor Allman wasn't happy about the World Army getting involved in the biology department's work. I could tell from the start."

She looked impressed, and then her eyes narrowed. "You're going to ask Professor Allman to help you infiltrate a high-level World Army scientist's workstation?"

I took a long draw off the blunt, poured smoke out of the side of my lips. "And he's going to say yes. Know why?"

She leaned forward. "Why?"

"Encantado magic."

CHAPTER TWENTY-ONE

I'd never been great at walking in heels. Today, I had to be genius.

When Serena Russo walked out of the biology building with her purse over her shoulder, I glanced at the time on my phone. 12:15 p.m.

I had one hour.

I was lucky to be her protege in the lab, to know she had a "lunch engagement" this afternoon and wouldn't be available to supervise my research.

Fine by me.

I walked into the biology building as soon as she'd disappeared around the corner and stepped into the first women's bathroom I encountered. I checked to be sure all the stalls were empty, and then locked the main door to start the inexpert process of turning into Serena Russo.

Well, not turning into her, precisely. Looking like her. Sounding like her.

This was going to hurt.

I took off all my clothes and stood in front of the mirror, pressing my red hair behind my ears and closing my eyes. Before the gods left, this used to be a giddy moment, as familiar to me as getting dressed in the morning.

Now I felt only dread.

Some days I would shift between three or four illusions between dawn and dusk. I could snap my fingers and my hair would tumble black, then brown, then red. I could blink and be blue-eyed, blink again and hazel, violet, gray. Whatever a man wanted. Whatever I felt like that day.

Since the gods left, I'd changed illusions four times. The first time was the day they departed, and I didn't understand how magic worked. I wanted to test the boundaries, to fully understand. The second time came two years later, when I decided I wanted to be the redhead I was now, a woman I'd seen at the airport in Montreal.

The third time, I became Katrina Darling. The litmus test was Justin, who never suspected I was anyone else. That was how good my illusions were.

And the fourth time, I un-became Katrina. I returned to the red-haired, green-eyed Isabella everyone in my life knew me as. The illusion that felt most like me. Going back was easy—because I'd already used it before, it only took five seconds off my life.

Going forward? That was the hard part.

I balled my hands to fists. I didn't want to look like Serena Russo, to burn two months off the end of my life just to spend lunchtime pretending to be a scientist who had sold herself to the World Army.

But hey, maybe I'd eaten enough Twinkies that my future, arterially-blocked self would be grateful for an early end. Or maybe, I thought as the familiar bubbling started in my gut, I was just trying to make the most of a shitty situation.

Shitty wasn't the right word.

Frightening. Depressing. Inviting the void.

Yes, those were the right words.

Once, I'd tried to describe to Aimee what it was like to burn time off my life. I'd compared it to approaching the edge of a cliff, beyond which was darkness. And burning time was like throwing yourself toward that edge.

"But we're all looking out over a cliff," Aimee said. "Humans and Others."

"Right," I said. "But imagine that, for five hundred years, there was no cliff. There was only a wide, rolling vista."

Her eyes grew big. "And then an earthquake happened."

"And then an earthquake happened," I whispered. But for me, the gods' departure wasn't an earthquake. It wasn't even a rumble. It was just that horn in the sky like a one-note tune, and then that voice pouring through the trees.

"Thank you for believing in us, but it is not enough. We're leaving. Good luck."

And after it had finished, the world settled onto me like a blanket. Where before the rainforest air had seemed refreshing, mortality brought an exhausting and throat-clutching humidity.

Mosquitos began biting. Leaves began to hurt my bare feet.

And all at once, illusions became a commodity. My life for the face I wanted.

I was trading my future for a little power. A little magic.

Four years of mortality wasn't enough time to get used to that.

Aimee tried, but she couldn't truly understand. It was impossible for humans, who'd been mortal from the time they understood their own existence. Every time Others used magic, we were sacrificing ourselves. We were inviting the void.

And for a OnceImmortal to do that, we had to be compelled by either life-threatening fear, or an overwhelming desire to do right.

This was me doing right.

I pictured Serena's black hair, the sheen of it. Her eyes. Her olive skin. Her long, coltish limbs. The magic thrilled me and sapped me all at once, my life force surging through me and floating away on a soft breeze. All the illusions of my long life flitted through my mind, the moments I'd stood in just this way, becoming someone else.

Except this time, I couldn't indulge. I only had fifteen minutes to make this illusion happen.

The cracking began as my bones separated, lengthened, stretching me out like a child's doll. My skull cracked, widened, reseamed, the bones of my face reshaping themselves more prominent, my chin jutting farther. I gritted through it as the muscles wound themselves over the new bones, and the skin over that.

When I opened my eyes, Serena Russo breathed hard in front of me. I gasped, one set of red fingernails rising to her mouth. She was me. I was the enemy.

I glanced around, felt almost dizzy. The world looked a lot different from six feet up. And I would have to get used to it—quick.

I grabbed my backpack, pulled out the pant suit and heels I'd bought last night. I had to estimate her size, and I'd nearly gotten it right. It was just a little loose through the arms and legs. The black heels cramped my toes, but I'd only need to wear them for the next—

I glanced down at my phone on the counter; a half hour had elapsed. GoneGodDamn, I'd lost my edge.

I pushed the backpack and my old clothes into a corner and clattered toward the bathroom door with the elegant little purse I'd brought. No time to practice—no time to do anything but go straight to the man I needed to see.

When I emerged from the bathroom, a gaggle of biology students stared at me. I recognized two of the girls from my classes, though they looked much shorter now. I gave them my best imperious look as I strode by, my toes protesting with every step.

I got into the elevator, took it to the third floor. When I stepped out, I spotted his door open, a yellow rectangle of light spilling out into the hallway.

Thank the GoneGods he was there.

Half a minute later, I stood at the threshold of his office, knocked politely on the door. "Prof—" I started. What was his first name? It had fled my mind. "Uh, Steve?"

Professor Allman glanced up from his desk. When his eyes lit on me, I sensed the familiar glint of attraction. *Really?* I thought. *Her?* I mean, she was beautiful, but she was also horrible.

But the body wants what the body wants. And I could use this to my advantage.

"Serena," he said, nearly tipping his chair over as he stood. Its wheels whined across the floor in one of the awkwardest demonstrations of male attraction I'd seen, and that was saying a lot. His hands rubbed on the front of his pants. "What a surprise. I thought you'd be out to lunch."

So he knew about her lunch engagement. Great.

I stepped forward, leaning lightly against the door. "It ended early. And silly me, when I got back, I realized I'd left my keycard at my workstation. Can't do much to help Others if I can't get into my work, can I?"

I set hopeful eyes on him.

Here it was: his chance to be a knight.

"Oh." His brow furrowed. "Security couldn't help you?"

Come on, Allman—I'm giving you an in.

I raised my shoulders. "They're out to lunch, too." I took another step forward. "Could you just swipe me in with yours?"

I knew his keycard would grant him access to Serena's workstation because he was the volunteer fire responder for the biology building. Every building had a do-gooder professor who'd volunteered to be the responder—to usher everyone out when the alarm sounded—and Professor Allman was that man. He was also the guy who wouldn't hesitate to help out.

Which was part of why I admired him so much.

He grabbed up his keycard off his desk, gesturing me into the hallway ahead of him. "Of course."

I grinned as I turned and stepped out. *Still got it.*

↔

Professor Allman swiped us through the lab's outer door, which gave two unusually pleasant chirps. I'd expected something more sinister, more ominous—two staccato klaxon bursts, maybe.

When we came inside, my eyes darted right to Serena's workstation. As before, the door was still shut. The keycard entry blinked red.

And then I noticed all the people; the lab bustled with an unpleasant number of researchers—way more than yesterday. I'd thought the lunch hour would mean everyone would clear out. But no, turns out scientists have a terrible sense of work/life balance. I should have known.

One lifted his head and approached me in a burst of recognition, what wisps remained of his blond hair blowing under the heating vent. He stood at least a foot shorter. "You're back," he said, lifting his face, "that was a quick meeting."

I nodded, pursed my lips. "You know how it goes."

He gave a knowing nod. "Do I." His eyes traveled to Professor Allman, who stood beside me. "Come to check in on your undergrads, Professor?"

The moment he'd said it, Professor Allman's face dropped a few degrees.

I ground my teeth at the condescension. Whoever this guy was, I wanted to tell him that Professor Allman was a brilliant biologist, and he had a 4.5 on the website RateMyProfessor—

"Actually, Serena forgot her keycard. I'm swiping her in," Allman said. He set a daring hand at my back—*go Steve!*—and guided me toward Serena's workstation.

As we walked, I glanced at my phone in my purse. I had twenty minutes remaining, and that was if she took the full hour. Given the way that scientist had looked at me after I'd said I cut the "meeting" short, I might not get that full twenty minutes.

"Here we go," Allman said, swiping his keycard. And with two more chirps, I was in.

I practically burst into her workstation, crossing behind the desk in two strides (Man, being tall had some perks). A stack of papers sat at one corner, which I lifted and began sifting through.

I needed to find that manila folder.

"You need anything else?" Professor Allman asked from the doorway, where he hovered in a bout of nervous fidgeting. "Coffee?"

I glanced up, my fingers still rifling through the papers. "I'm good. Thanks, Steve." I added a wink, and I swear, I might have made the man's knees wobble.

Ah, if only I could tell him how truly evil I was. Well, how evil Serena was. Maybe another time, after I'd done what I needed to do.

He disappeared out of the doorway, and my search became less dignified. I set my thumb on the edge of the pile and flicked through it. No folder.

I straightened, spun in a half-circle. To my left sat an elegant white filing cabinet with three drawers. I pulled open the top one. Empty. I pulled open the middle one.

Bingo. Manila folders.

Except there were about thirty of them.

I reached in, grabbing up the closest one. When I opened it, an image of something horrific stared back at me. It looked like a woman's head, but with tentacles for a body. A different Other, but with a full file of documentation.

And probably an unfertilized embryo in a petri dish somewhere in this lab.

I put the file back in, moved to the next one. Another Other, this one also female, but with the lower body of an arachnid. Arachne.

Each file I looked at contained female Others, most of them stupidly powerful.

When I'd gone through eight files, I reached into my purse to see my phone. I had ten minutes. When I glanced over my shoulder, everything seemed as normal. No other Serena—yet.

Five more files. More Others. I pushed the second drawer shut, opened the third drawer.

Even more manila folders.

And it occurred to me: why was ultra-classified information like this being kept on paper? It should be locked away on a computer. Well, it probably was, but Serena Russo was a technophobe.

I had noticed it right away. She didn't have a computer. She didn't carry a smartphone or a tablet. She wore a wristwatch. When she and Allman had set up a meeting in my presence, she had written it in a paper planner.

If you were working for the World Army, technologically-averse was a terrible thing to be. Especially when one overly curious encantado decided to stick her nose in.

After three more folders, I finally found Empusa's.

I had five minutes left, which meant I had to move fast. I shut the door and laid the file open on Serena's desk. I pulled out my phone from my purse and started taking pictures.

Then I heard it: tap-tap, tap-tap. Those heels.

"Serena," came a muffled voice, "you surprised me."

I spent a second frozen, and then I flicked my phone over to text messages, shot off my pre-written text. It disappeared into the ether, and a second later read as *delivered.*

I only had two bars of reception. *Please*, I thought like a teenager waiting for her crush to acknowledge her text. *Please.*

I closed the folder, set it in the drawer and pressed it silently shut. Then I ducked down and waited. And prayed to the GoneGods for a miracle.

Tap-tap. Tap-tap.

Serena's shadow was at the door. She was rustling in her purse.

A swipe, and the double-chirp of the keycard entry. With that, the door began to open and I wondered if waterboarding would be effective on an encantado in her natural form.

But I wasn't going to find out—not today.

With a burst of sound and light, the fire alarm went off. Somewhere in the building, Steve Allman was rushing to find his volunteer fire responder vest. But here in the biology lab, Serena let the door shut, and I was again alone in her office.

"*Obrigado,*" I whispered. *Thank you, thank you.*

I had minutes at most. Fortunately, resuming an old illusion wasn't nearly as taxing—or as time-consuming—as taking on a new one.

Thirty seconds later, I rolled the hems of my fancy pant suit up so I could run barefooted out of Serena Russo's office. I pushed my red hair out of my face as I navigated past the empty workstations and out of the lab, which had cleared at once.

Ahh, the good old threat of burning alive. Worked every time.

I ran down the hall and into the bathroom. I changed into my regular clothes and came out at a jog, bursting through the main doors of the biology building and crossing down the steps toward Aimee.

"Another stupid fire drill," I said, turning back to look up at the building.

She rolled her eyes. "What a waste of time."

CHAPTER TWENTY-TWO

*W*e dropped into our chairs, and I set my phone on the table between Aimee and me. My hands trembled at either side of it.

"I don't think it's safe enough here." I glanced around the little deli we'd ducked into after leaving the biology building. We were only a couple blocks from the scene of our crime, and I was pretty sure the *tap-tap* of Dr. Russo's shoes was going to be a trauma-trigger for the rest of my mortal life.

"Isa, there's no one here except us."

I pointed. "And that guy behind the counter."

She glanced over her shoulder. "He's got earbuds in. And he's jamming out."

The Brazilian in me surfaced. "Well, I don't know about that."

"OK." She sighed. "He's shuffling his feet and bobbing his head. Happy?"

I nodded, forcing a little smile. Faking it was making it, right? Even if I felt like a live wire on the inside.

"So, are you going to look at the pictures?" Aimee said.

I turned on the phone and unlocked it. As soon as I did, the last image I'd taken appeared on the screen. Aimee angled her head, and the two of us read what I'd captured from Empusa's file, picture by picture.

When we got to the page detailing how to neutralize her, our gazes locked. "Holy shit," Aimee said. "This is proof right here the World Army was behind this."

"But why?" My eyes flicked back to the phone, then to Aimee. "Why would they do this on a college campus? There are more humans here than Others—in fact …"

"It's all humans," Aimee said.

"What is?"

"Everyone who's been murdered. Not a single Other."

My mouth hung open. She was right: at least four murders (that we knew of), and all Other-on-human. Not one instance of Other-on-Other. And while humans did outnumber Others in Montreal, if I had to guess at Empusa's ratio if she were allowed to go on killing, it would remain 1:0.

All humans, no Others.

"They're trying to instill fear of Others," I said. "That's why Tremblay wasn't taking me seriously."

"Who's Tremblay?"

"The officer at the police station. He's been in contact with the World Army."

"Isn't Justin a cadet with them, too?"

A needle pierced my chest; I set a hand there. "Yes."

"Do you think …?"

"No," I said. "He doesn't know about the connection between Empusa and the World Army. He's not part of this."

Her blue eyes stayed fast on me. "Are you sure?"

I slid my phone off the table, clicked the screen off. "I'm sure." I dropped it into my purse, reached for my jacket.

"What are you doing now?"

"I'm going to work," I said. "I'm supposed to be in the lab."

"If you were going to work, you would have looked at me when you said that."

GoneGodDamn, she knew me well. I raised my eyes. "It's not dark

165

yet."

"Don't go after her, Isa. You and I both read what she's capable of, and you're not an Other-slayer."

"Maybe not." I rose from my seat. "But I know birds."

She walked with me out of the deli and down the sidewalk. "Where are you going?"

The blessing and the curse of having a best friend: they don't mind being clingy when they sense you're about to do something dangerous.

"The butcher's shop."

"Uh ... aren't you a pescatarian?"

"Yes."

"You do realize butchers only deal in non-fish?"

"Yes."

"Can you give me something more than monosyllabic answers?"

"Well, give me something besides a yes/no question." I was being difficult, and I knew it.

She threw her hands in the air. "Isa, why are you going to the butcher's shop? I'm really nervous that you're about to do something stupid."

"I can't tell you," I said. I didn't stop walking. "I'm sorry, Aimee."

"Come on, without me you wouldn't have gotten out of Serena's office in one piece. You'd probably be in a World Army camp with a bag over your head or something."

She was right, but that didn't change things. I stopped, turning to her. Like mine, her cheeks were red and chapped from the winter wind. "Thank you for saving my behind, but please go home. I know you'll get involved if I tell you more."

"I won't."

"You will."

She knew I knew, and she stamped her foot on the sidewalk and glanced around. "Swear you'll text me tonight," she said. "If you don't come back to the dorm, text me to let me know you're all right."

I set a hand on my chest, the other raised in the air. "I swear."

A minute later, Aimee was walking back toward our dorm, and I stood alone and frigid on the sidewalk. Right up until she'd gone I had felt annoyed by her presence, and now I regretted sending her away.

I was about to do something very, very stupid. And I was about to do it without anyone else's help. At this point, I didn't know who to trust, and beyond that, I didn't want to get anyone hurt if this ended up not working.

"It'll work," I whispered as I stepped into the butcher's shop. I knew birds—it would work, even if these birds were older than the Bible.

Even monsters from antiquity needed to eat.

I beelined for the counter, where meathooks pierced massive slabs of who-knew-what; I tried not to look too closely. "Hello," I said to the man behind the counter, who was busily cleaving into a hunk of red flesh. His apron looked like he'd killed a cow right in his lap. "I'd like sixty pounds of pig, please."

He lifted his face and set his massive cutting knife on the board. He didn't say anything.

"Uh, do you sell pig?" I said.

"I sell pig."

"I'll take sixty pounds."

"I heard you the first time. We sell it in one-pound increments."

"Well, I'll take sixty one-pound increments. In one bag, please."

The dull eyes opened wide. "How will you even carry all that?"

"I'm an Other," I said, like that explained it all.

"Oh." And then, without further question, he started preparing my pig. Thirty minutes later, he'd filled a bag of meat so well he could hardly lift it off the ground. He set it on the counter and rang me up. "That'll be three hundred and twenty dollars. Do you need help getting it to your car?"

"Nope." I hauled the bag back onto my shoulder and turned toward the door. He didn't say anything, and I realized then how little most humans actually knew about Others, how much they accepted as gospel just based on someone's word.

The truth was, being an encantado didn't give me any extra

strength. Lifting barbells at the gym had done that—just like it would for any human.

And my knowledge about birds? Yes, I had spent five hundred years among them in the rainforest. But that was a subset of birds I'd been exposed to; I knew about species around the world because of my interest and the hours I'd spent reading, like anyone else would. Any human, any Other.

But what I was about to do … Well, that might qualify as unique encantado recklessness. We were, after all, prone to acting on impulse.

CHAPTER TWENTY-THREE

*W*hen I was immortal, I lived near a small village of humans by the Amazon River. The village had always been slow to develop; until well into the 20th century, it remained small and insular and singularly superstitious.

In this village, encantado were creatures to be feared. And for good reason: we had a tendency to steal away with their young men. For our part, it wasn't totally conscious or malicious ... we just became infatuated.

Deeply, obsessively so.

It wasn't like human limerence. Our infatuations ran deeper, consumed us so well that if we hadn't been immortal, we might have combusted from lack of nutrition or sleep or—almost inevitably— broken hearts. We were like the Juliets of Others, except our romances weren't cut short by poisoning or suicide after three days.

Well, at least not for our part. It was the Romeos who tended to be problematic. But they just kept appearing, and we just kept falling for them.

In the village, the men developed a ritual. As a test of manhood, they ventured into the rainforest in search of our home. My community was a small, matriarchal cluster—encantado are never created male—a kilometer's walk away. We hadn't built traditional structures; by and large, we lived under the rain and the sun, swam in the river every day. When we slept, it was on the grass. When we ate, we caught fish from the river and respectfully consumed every part.

No waste. No destruction.

We were among the original environmentalists.

The only true markers of our home were the clothes we hung on branches, what we would change into when we took on our illusions. It was our nature which kept us near the human world, our eternal desire for love and fantasy.

So we didn't mind the ritual. In fact, we relished it, each of us taking our turns appearing to the villagers who reached our home.

Of course, some men turned back early. Some didn't find us at all. But those who did had to approach us like the sirens of Greek lore, to resist what they saw and heard and return to the village as men.

Some found us and never returned to the village. Some of those men became mine—for a time.

But only one of those men ever loved me. Really, truly. His name was Marco.

He came to our home in the forest, and I was the first encantado he met. A young, naked woman, brown curls lapping over my shoulder and down my chest. And though I didn't cover myself, he didn't take his eyes off mine. We talked and walked and before he left to return to the village, he kissed me on the cheek. I was charmed, but I didn't expect him to come back.

It was the encantado who chose to follow her Romeo, if she desired. It was the encantado who stole her man of choice from the village.

But the next day, he returned. And because I wasn't infatuated with him, I didn't show myself. He met other encantado, but none were me, and he wanted none of them.

He only wanted the first one. Isabella.

He returned the next day, and the next. And though I never showed myself to him, he returned. Unflagging, unflappable Marco, calling my name through the trees.

Then he brought the seed.

On that morning I woke to birdcall, delighted laughter. The sun pierced the trees in wells of light, and in those pockets, the Amazonian birds flitted back and forth with mouthfuls of seed. Big and small, common and rare, the brilliant and the dull-feathered species together.

I had never seen so many birds in one place, never seen them intermingle that way. And all it had taken was birdseed, spread and offered on the ground.

Among them stood Marco, both hands outstretched like Lady Justice, birdseed in the flats of his palms. And that was when I understood the spark versus the slow-burn, the match versus the kindling.

I walked to Marco, took up a handful of seed, and didn't leave his side for the next forty years.

He taught me important truths: first impressions aren't always ironclad. Acting on impulse isn't mutually exclusive with exercising judgment.

And if you ever want to bring all the birds to the yard, don't forget the grub.

↔

I stepped into the white tree line of Mont Royal, the city slung low behind me and the bag still heavy over my shoulder. In my periphery, the sun demanded attention, willing me to turn my head left for a single, retina-scalding moment.

Above, the branches rose iced and otherwise bare toward the sky. No birds, but also no creatures. Nothing moved around me except what the wind blew into motion, and though I hadn't entered this forest before, I knew that wasn't right.

In an hour, darkness would envelop this dormant forest. In an hour, Empusa would be dead. She wouldn't get another night to kill— not one more human, not one more death.

I crunched through the leaves, trekking deeper. When I had gotten a half-mile in, I heard the first caw before I spotted it.

I cringed, my ears ringing as I lifted my eyes to the high canopy. A single stymphalian bird, cocking its head to gaze black-eyed back at me.

No—not just one. The longer I looked, the more I saw. Two, three, five, eight. Another caw, and all at once the whole flock was riled to motion, sweeping up into the air in a vortex. My hair blew up around my face, and I knew if I moved at all, I would lose my nerve. I would run.

Half a minute later, they settled into lethargy. It was daytime, after all—well, at least for a little while.

I dropped the bag to the ground, pulled my keys from my pocket and ripped open the top. At once the scent hit me, and it hit them, too. I tried not to retch as they screeched.

"Hey boys." I ungloved one hand to the frigid air. I reached into the bag and sank my fingers into the bloody mess. I tried not to retch—we encantados were pescatarians, after all—as I pulled out a handful of pig guts. "Dinner's come early."

I raised the meat aloft, gesturing up at the cyclone of birds before I threw the whole of it on the ground. All at once, their flight pattern changed; where before they'd circled with purpose, now they descended with distinct—and terrifying—intent.

Birds of prey were birds of prey. I knew they liked man-meat, but it seemed pig meat worked just as well. Before they got too close, I grabbed up the bag and jogged ten feet, plunging my hand in again and again, littering the ground with meat as I went.

As the first swooped down behind me, it let a screech so awful I ducked my head, my whole body freezing. I would probably have permanent tinnitus after this was all over.

Keep going. Keep going, Isabella. I forced myself to straighten, to continue on as I reached into the bag for more meat. I trailed it along the ground, not looking back.

At any moment one could swoop in and end me with its beak or talons, but I knew from Empusa's file that they had a directive: don't kill humans. Of course, I didn't know how well it applied to Others with a human illusion, or how effective it was in the face of an Other whose hands were covered in pig gore.

So far they hadn't come for me, and I kept moving deeper into the forest with their terrible noises following behind.

After three minutes, I heard a different call. It sounded like terror.

I spun around, my eyes following the uneven flight of one of the stymphalian birds as it careened over the tree line. It called out, dropped a few feet and swerved to miss a few branches before it crashed headlong into the trunk of a tree.

The tree shuddered as its black body dropped straight down the length of the trunk and landed on the ground in a crash of leaves. And for a moment, silence enveloped the forest.

I didn't move; I couldn't. The whole scene felt so quiet, so surreal, that I wondered if I had dreamed all of this in the same way I'd dreamed of El Lobizon so many nights afterward. Every time waking up, every time immobile in my bed with my heart hammering.

A rumble started through the forest, growing in volume and intensity. Not the birds, because after a few seconds, they too chimed in, landing on the branches around their dead flockmate to cast their faces skyward and call toward the sky.

A second later, another stymphalian bird dropped, hit the ground with an inelegant thud. The rumble rose from a baritone to an alto, and then to a soprano howling that went on and on.

I turned, my hand still full of pig. There he stood: the hunter. El Lobizon, his canines gleaming in the new moonlight as he howled into the sky not fifty feet from me.

You see, I had expected Empusa. A woman missing maybe a leg, or an arm. Maybe her face would be covered in blood or her eyes wouldn't close. She would hop or walk toward me, and I would keep spreading the poisoned meat onto the ground because she could not hurt me.

When this moment came, I'd planned to talk myself out of fear. I'd planned to carry on a conversation with myself that would be so casual I would somehow trick my brain and nervous system into believing what was occurring around me shouldn't incur mortal terror. I wasn't at risk of death.

But I hadn't expected El Lobizon.

All at once, I remembered again what the museum placard had said. *Empusa is a shapeshifter who plays on your fears, often taking the form of that which frightens you the most.*

El Lobizon the hunter, the wolf, frightened me the most.

I opened my mouth, but I couldn't make the words come.

It's Empusa, not the hunter.

It's not El Lobizon, Isa. Focus on what you know about Empusa.

It wasn't in her directive to hurt a woman. And her power was tied in with the birds, which were dropping one by one. But not fast enough—at least forty birds still remained—because the massive wolf before me lowered its face, those golden eyes shifting to me and lips rising into a snarl that I knew meant my death.

I was killing her. When it came to her directive, all bets were off. Empusa would end me if she could.

El Lobizon began stalking toward me, enormous paws setting divots the size of my entire body into the ground. I couldn't help but look down at those claws, surveying the left forepaw. *Five* claws—not four. Which meant Empusa didn't know my secret.

El Lobizon soon set into a run, and still I was stuck to the spot where I stood.

She can hurt you, even if she's not the real hunter. She can still kill you.

Forty feet.

Move, Isa.

Twenty feet.

Move, move, move!

Ten feet.

Move or die!

As Empusa reached me, I threw myself out of the way, those enormous jaws snapping in my wake. I hit the ground hard, rolling twice before a tree trunk stopped me.

Yes, she could hurt me. She could kill me.

I raised my head; behind us, another bird fell. Not fast enough.

The poison I'd concocted had been potent enough to bring down elephants, but apparently stymphalian birds were tougher than that.

So many still remained. And they were now flying toward me, protecting their mistress. What I'd read in that manila folder in Serena Russo's office had explained so much about the birds' behavior.

Somehow, the World Army had fractured Empusa's power and siphoned it into the entire flock of birds, with whom she bore an invisible connection. That meant she could control them like a hive mother.

It also meant their fate was her fate. If they were poisoned, she was poisoned.

I flicked my gaze back to where Empusa had been, but the forest was empty. I pushed myself halfway up, scanning the darkening forest. I caught a glimpse of a tail disappearing behind a tree trunk, but no wolf appeared on the other side.

Instead, a woman emerged. She ran on her hands and feet, faster even than a dog or a wolf—more like the girl from *The Ring* on uppers.

And she was coming toward me.

CHAPTER TWENTY-FOUR

I was alone. Completely, stupidly alone.

Behind me, avian death. Ahead, monster death. Empusa ran at me with a mop of black, matted hair, the mouth of her pale face open wide as her slender arms pulled her through the forest.

I had nowhere to run. And I was going to die covered in pig blood.

I thought of Aimee, back there in our dorm, probably cozy in her checkered pajamas. Of Justin, in the O³ house, practicing his cute-yet-terrifying World Army salute. Both of them wouldn't be in this situation in the first place, because they were smart. They had common sense.

I was the oldest of the three of us, and I had none, apparently.

And I thought: *This was a mistake. This was a terrible plan.*

But as Empusa came toward me, someone pulled me to my feet. No—not someone.

Me.

I had pulled me to my feet. I was reaching into my backpack and yanking out El Lobizon's claw. I had wrapped its edge in leather, gripped the makeshift hilt in my fist and leaned toward Empusa.

For the first time in five hundred years, I understood that you couldn't always escape using glamour or guise. That sometimes you had to fight. I was no fighter, but I also wasn't going to go down easy.

"Monte de merda!" I yelled, gesturing with my free hand.

Empusa didn't stop. She didn't slow. Instead, she let a violent hiss as she barreled toward me.

Well, that phrase had worked on catcalling assholes back in Brazil.

A stymphalian bird swooped down behind me, and I felt something yank hard on my hair. Damn bird was trying to stop me from running—not that its plan worked. I pulled hard as I kept moving, the roots of my hair tearing away in a patch of red tendrils. It flew another twenty feet before it rose in an arc and nosedived straight into the leaves with a *thwump!*

I glanced over my shoulder and ducked just in time to avoid two more birds making a pass. Four feathers *thwacked!* like bulletfire into the tree trunk beside me.

When I turned back, Empusa was in front of me.

She swerved left before she reached me, and I realized she was predicting the direction I'd jumped last time. I tried to dive right, but an iron vise gripped my ankle and dragged me across the leaves and up into the air.

She held me up like she was inspecting a feral, swinging cat. From this view, she looked even uglier. But GoneGodDamn was she strong.

Around us, the forest burst into stymphalian cries, the birds swooping closer, my hair blowing around my head as their wings beat hard.

Her free hand reached out, the fingers tipped with three-inch long claws. Even as I could scent her weakening, it was a measured, confident reach—an assured kill.

Wait for it, Isa. Wait.

The hand came closer, revealed in the moments when my hair wasn't blown in front of my eyes. She was going for my heart.

Right for the heart.

When she'd come to within two inches, I raised the claw and swiped it across her wrist. A small cut, but El Lobizon's claws didn't need to cut deep. It stopped her hand at once. As her black blood seeped from the cut, it began to smoke.

Her magic began seeping out of her wrist like air from a balloon.

She could shapeshift into El Lobizon, but evidently she didn't know his power: the nullification of magic. Those claws were an Other's worst nightmare.

She hissed so loudly I dropped the feather. But she didn't drop me.

Instead, her wounded hand jerked toward me with impossible speed.

GoneGods be good—I was going to die after all.

I closed my eyes. And for a second, I went somewhere else.

I rewound to the moment I'd met Justin.

When you've lived hundreds of years, you become a daydreamer, a thinker. If you don't, you go crazy—immortal life is just too long to live with human freneticism. And you gain an incredible capacity to disappear inside yourself. To remember the moments of your life with cinematic clarity.

If I was going to die remembering one moment, I wanted it to be when I met Justin. Not as Kat—not when I'd pretended to be his girl-friend walking toward him in the dining hall.

No, just as Isabella. Just as me, a mortal.

"What are you doing?" he'd asked.

I glanced up from where I sat in front of my microscope, squinting at the halo of fluorescent light behind his head. That was the first time we met: his shadowed head under the ceiling light, the two of us unknown to each other.

"Studying DNA," I said. "Are you supposed to be in here?"

He half-smirked and leaned on the counter beside me. "Probably not."

Now his face became real, and I understood he was the same guy I'd seen so many times in our dorm, walking with the five-foot-nothing freshman called Katrina Darling. Black-haired, blue-eyed, a little swagger. The same one I'd ascribed so many fantasies to: his coolness, how dashing he'd be if I were in trouble, the way he pushed his hair behind his ear.

Those blue eyes moved like the sea in front of me, and I almost forgot my annoyance at him touching the workstation I kept ultra clean. At him being here in the first place. *Jaguar,* I thought for the first time. *Kingdom: Animalia. Genus: Panthera. Class: Mammalia. Species: P. onca.*

"Are you a researcher?" I asked.

He laughed. A totally genuine, unaffected laugh right from his belly. "No—I'm just a guy who's lost."

That humility surprised me.

I stood. "Where do you need to be?"

He extended a crumpled slip of paper—a class schedule. "Room 114B."

"Oh." I led him out of the lab. "That's an easy mistake to make. This is 114R, which is the research area adjacent to 114."

He smiled. "My mistake."

As we came into the hall, another guy who'd been standing there raised his eyes. He looked nervous, and avoided meeting my gaze. But he'd clearly been waiting for Justin.

"It's 114B, man," Justin said as he passed him pack the slip of crumpled paper.

The other guy booked it for 114B, and Justin started down the hall in the opposite direction.

I turned after Justin. "Hey."

He glanced over his shoulder.

I pointed behind me. "Your class is that way."

"It's all good. Thanks for your help." He passed down the hallway, and I stared after him.

What was that all about?

Later, I would learn that Justin wasn't even enrolled in the class in room 114B. It was the nervous guy who'd been waiting in the hallway. He had a severe stutter and social anxiety, and Justin—a passerby— was just helping him out.

Now, months later, I knew for certain that my fantasies about Justin weren't all true. But he was kind. And if five hundred years had taught me anything, it was to keep the kind ones close.

↔

Empusa's claws touched my jacket, and just when I thought this was it, a voice cried out. I knew that voice.

"Isabella!"

I opened my eyes, which blurred with tears. I wasn't alone.

A thud vibrated through my ankle, and Empusa dropped me with another world-splitting scream. I hit the ground so hard I wasn't sure if I'd been hit or she had, but when I looked up, an arrow stuck like a sign marker out the side of her head.

Another followed, the lethal arrowhead disappearing into her chest.

I turned my face left, blinking hard at the flurry of motion before me. The birds floated, circled, flapped, screeched. They dropped with arrows protruding from their bodies. They fell with their wings cleft by swords.

In the center stood a group of humans, their weapons gleaming in the quarter-light.

The World Army cadets.

As I thought it, one of them emerged from the fray with a bow in one hand and an arrow in the other. His face was shadowed by the fresh moonlight, a white halo behind him, but I didn't need to see his features to know who he was.

"Isabella—move!" he yelled.

I rolled off my back and dug my hands into the leaves as my feet sought purchase, pulling myself away from Empusa without one look back. Every fiber of me ached toward Justin, who was anchoring his next arrow in the heavy-duty bow.

Since when does he know archery?

Don't ask questions, dummy—just move!

I finally got my feet under me, running toward him. He seemed to be aiming straight at me, but I knew he was focused past me. Even so, just before he loosed the arrow with a whistle, I strafed left.

Hey, he may have been good enough to hit Empusa twice, but I knew he hadn't been practicing archery for more than about a month. I wasn't about to risk it.

When I reached his side, I spun around behind him. "I got her with El Lobizon's claw," I breathed. "The birds are poisoned."

"I know." Justin nocked his next arrow.

I stared at the back of his head. Had he been watching me? Did he know what I'd done with the meat and the claw? But there wasn't time to wonder, because ahead of us, Empusa had dropped to all fours, her mouth wide open in a hiss. Three arrows stuck out of her at odd angles, and a thin stream of black blood issued from each of them.

But she still hadn't fallen. GoneGodDamn she was powerful.

"That's her attack stance," I said. "She's about to come at us."

"Not with an arrow in her face, she isn't." Justin drew the bowstring taut, and as Empusa launched into motion—well, I knew what I would be seeing in my nightmares for the rest of my mortal life —he let the arrow go.

It flew through the air in a perfect line, and like a perfect half-court shot, the glinting arrowhead disappeared into her mouth.

Just as Justin had predicted, her head jerked back, and her upper body with it. She slid ten feet across the ground before stopping in a heap, the arrow in her mouth jutting vertical into the air.

It was the perfect shot. A shot worthy of Paris the Trojan prince, or Katniss Everdeen. A shot that one in a thousand expert archers could make, and Justin had made it. Easily. *That shouldn't be possible,* I thought, remembering the coin that he'd caught mid-air. I was both worried about Justin's sudden abilities and grateful that he had them.

Before us, Empusa didn't move.

Behind us, a whoop went up. We turned in time to see the rest of the birds drop to the ground in a pile around the World Army soldiers, who stood in the middle of what looked like a frozen forest. Around them, feathers glinted like icicles in the trees.

"That was ... Woah." Justin dropped his bow to reach for me. I only realized when his hands went around me that my legs had given out like matchsticks.

I wanted to hug him. To tell him how crazy and stupid and reckless that was. To ask him when the hell he had learned to shoot like that.

But my autonomic system had taken over, and my lungs pressed air in and out with mechanical persistence. I had never hyperventilated before, and even as I realized what was happening, it was still a new, completely mortal thing. As a biologist I knew how much actual control mortals had over their bodies (much less than we liked to think), but it was still terrifying to experience.

"It's OK, Isa." Justin's warm hands slid over me, his body a weighted blanket pressing around me. How was he so good at this?

"I—" I tried between breaths. "I—"

"I know," he said. "I know."

So I stopped trying, allowed myself to be enveloped. To be held and comforted. And soon enough my breathing slowed, normalized. I raised my eyes, found Justin looking down at me.

The same look as the first time we met.

"Back away from the creature," came Sergeant Johnson's voice from ahead. "Police are on their way." He stepped past Justin and me, staring down at Empusa.

The two of us stood together, passing into the crowd of cadets, all of whom stared on.

"We got it good," Johnson said, circling at a safe distance. "We got it good, boys."

It.

Empusa had been a female. A *she.* She was a murderer who had deserved death, but I also knew what had been inside that file. Her directive. Empusa had been a pawn of the World Army. I felt sure, had she not been tasked with mayhem, the outcome of her release into Montreal could have been different. Better.

Which made this scene—her dead in the dirt, all the stymphalian birds hacked to pieces—almost too tragic to bear.

"Let's go," I whispered to Justin.

I expected him to want to stay, and I'd end up leaving alone or with him only after some cajoling. To his credit, he squeezed my shoulder and we stepped away from the crowd.

We walked through the forest together, my arms around his waist, and emerged from the tree line to the nighttime vista of Montreal. Below us, the city glittered with what seemed to me a bright-eyed sense of safety. Of security.

The world wasn't fixed, not by a long shot. But there would be no more deaths—not by Empusa's hand.

He turned to me. "Want to come back to the house and get cleaned up?"

I lifted my face and said with complete, innocent sincerity, "There's nothing I want more."

It was true; especially because we needed to have a serious talk.

CHAPTER TWENTY-FIVE

*H*e had parked not far from Mont Royal, a short walk down the hill. By the time I climbed into Justin's car, I could hardly feel my hands. And when the interior light flicked on, I found myself covered in blood.

My hands. My jacket. My pants.

He didn't seem fazed. When he sat down next to me, he reached to set his hand at the back of my head.

"Wait," I said. "Don't touch me. The blood is poisoned."

His hand dropped. "Poisoned?"

"Arsenic. I laced the meat and blood with it."

"So that's why the birds were flying in figure-8s by the time we got there. Where did you get arsenic?"

"I made it in the lab."

"I thought you were a biologist."

"I've also lived five hundred years," I said. "I know a few things."

He nodded, didn't question me any further. Justin started the car, and we drove toward the O^3 house with the heat blasting, baking the arsenic-loaded blood onto my skin. I tried not to touch anything.

"How did you know?" I asked.

"Know what?"

"Where to go—how to find her? How to find me?"

"Sergeant Johnson got a tip. We were on patrol, and we made straight for the trees."

A tip. What a funny thing, that the World Army had unleashed Empusa and one of their sergeants would lead his soldiers to defeat her.

"From who?" I said.

He shrugged. "I didn't ask. We just geared up and moved."

"But how did you know how to fight her?"

Justin paused as the car came to a light, and we idled. "You know, I didn't ask about that, either. We just grabbed the weapons that Johnson told us to, and he briefed us about how the fight would go down on the way."

I stared at him, and he finally turned his face toward me. I could see his thoughts written all across it.

"You think I'm a drone," he said. "That I just do what I'm told."

I shook my head, but I didn't open my mouth to deny it, either. I should have, but I didn't. I turned back toward the windshield as the light turned.

"Isa," Justin said.

"Light's green."

He drove, and we arrived at the O^3 house in silence. When I stepped out of Justin's car, he came around and tried to take my hand.

"I'm still bloody, remember?" I said.

"Right—let's get you into a shower."

I nodded, but I didn't move.

"What is it?" He waited, his breath visible in white puffs as he watched me untangle my thoughts.

"Doesn't Sergeant Johnson need you at the scene?"

"Empusa's gone."

"I know, but … he said the police were coming. We should have stayed."

Justin stepped closer. "The threat's gone. We can go to the station tomorrow and tell them everything we know."

For the first time, I took in his clothing. He was wearing some sort of uniform with a logo on the breast. I nearly touched it, my fingers hovering over the outline. "The World Army. Does this mean you're a recruit?"

"I'm a volunteer for now."

I turned my eyes up. "For now?"

"Let's go inside, Isa. It's freezing out here."

I didn't move.

"I thought you wanted to come back with me," he said, finally getting annoyed. "If you don't want to talk about what's really on your mind, I can take you back to your dorm."

I stepped back, leaned against the icy car. Frigid metal seeped through my clothing, but I didn't move away. "I'm afraid," I said. "I nearly died tonight—and would have, if not for you. There are things I can't tell you about my research, but they scare me. And you ... you're with the World Army."

"I'm with you, Isabella."

My sight blurred. "There's a wedge."

"What wedge?"

"Between you and me."

He stepped closer. "I don't feel a wedge."

"I'm an Other," I whispered. "You just killed an Other."

"I killed an Other who was killing people. You haven't killed anyone. You're good, Isa."

"I've done bad things. I've tricked humans—I tricked you. I made men love me and then left them. Where do you draw the line, Justin, when you already hate Others?"

He sucked air. "Hate Others?"

I nodded, the warm tear slipping down my cheek a brief comfort.

He came to stand in front of me, and his hands found mine. "Don't," I said. "The blood."

"I'll wash it off," he murmured.

And I stopped resisting, because his hands felt like the heat off an oven. He pulled me away from the side of the car, and we stood pressed against one another in the driveway while he kissed my hair.

I cried. I finally, really cried. And the whole while, he stroked me and whispered I don't know what, but it sounded like the most comforting story I'd ever heard. I didn't want it to stop.

When the crying slowed, his fingers came under my chin and lifted it. "Isa, I don't hate Others. I can't—because you're one."

I let a single sob, and because I didn't have blood on my face, I allowed him to kiss me.

It was the best kiss of my long, long life.

So we walked toward the house together, his arm around me. And as we came around the side and up the walkway, a voice spoke up.

"Justin?"

We stopped before the front steps as a petite figure rose from the stoop, her face shrouded.

I knew that voice. It had once been my voice, for a time.

Justin didn't let go of my hand, but he very nearly did. He didn't speak, either, as the figure stepped forward and the porch light flicked on.

"Well," she said, surveying the scene from him to me. Her eyes lingered on me, then returned to him. "It looks like you've been busy."

Katrina Darling was back.

26

EPILOGUE

*I*f there's one thing Serena Russo loves, it's a snoop. They're the easiest to blackmail.

Kilby finds her at her workstation, and he tries hard not to show his attraction. But then, she encourages it: it's a large part of his loyalty—of any man's loyalty. And for as long as you've got it, you drink that milkshake dry.

"Dr. Russo." His head pokes through her door. Requesting permission to enter.

Serena's lips curl before she gestures him forward. "Come in, Kilby."

He steps inside, seems to bodily unfurl when the door shuts. He isn't good at playing the part of a low-level research assistant. He can't fit into any of the lab coats properly, and they only reach his knees. He's too bald to blend with the students. And there's something about him...

Something eternally creepy. Humans and Others sense it at once.

They stare at one another for a beat before her hand sweeps across the length of her desk. "Someone's been here."

He nods. "I know."

"Tell me what you know."

She sits back, arms folded under her chest, while Kilby explains. He watched her leave for her lunch-hour meeting, mysteriously reappear after only a half hour with Steve Allman in tow, and make straight for her workstation. Then she disappeared inside for the next fifteen minutes. When Serena—the real Serena—came into the lab a second time, "that," Kilby says, pressing a finger to her desk, "was when I knew."

"Because there were two of me, Kilby? Was that how you knew?"

He doesn't catch her tone of voice, or ignores it. He points to his wrist, where an old-fashion watch glistens under the fluorescents. "Time sped up."

Serena nods, and he continues his narration. The fire alarm began, and he stayed where he was. He waited, crouched in shadow. Kilby has always been her best man when it comes to lurking.

"And out she came, wearing your clothes," he says.

"She?"

"The sophomore researcher—the one studying the triple helix."

"The encantado," she says when he finishes. Serena sits up straight; she feels lit from the inside, her mind working fast. "How wonderful."

Kilby looks confused. "The what?"

"It doesn't matter." That is, it doesn't matter to Kilby. He's just her eyes—not her intelligence. "She's a snoop."

This is his language she's speaking, and he nods fast. "Definitely a snoop."

"Did you follow her?"

"Into the hallway."

"And?"

"She ducked into the nearest bathroom and came out in clothes that fit her."

"Then?"

"She left the building and ran into the crowd."

Perfect. "Tell me we've got video, Kilby."

That familiar look of pleasure crosses Stein's face—he knows he has what I desire. He can make me happy. "We've got video."

She sits forward, both elbows touching the desk as she stares up at him. "No, Kilby. We don't."

His pleasure vanishes, a tortured uncertainty replacing it. When did she begin to love these small manipulations? "We don't have video."

"That's right," Serena says. "You know it's policy to erase all the data after twenty-four hours. The university would be very angry with us for violating that part of our agreement."

Now he understands. He nods, and because the silence weighs too heavily, he turns to go.

"But," she says, "you'll send me what you saw."

He's already partly opened the door, and now he turns toward her, the low-level lab assistant once more. And even as she knows he's wearing those hi-tech contacts, it's hard to believe; he squints like a mole in the sun.

He taps one finger beside his left eye. "Yes, Dr. Russo." He pauses. "The trainee is waiting outside."

"Send him in, Kilby."

Then he's gone, and Serena is alone once more with Isabella Ramirez's file. She opens it, pens a note next to her species. *Encantado illusion fooled Kilby. Extremely powerful. Worthwhile female candidate for testing.*

Half a minute later, a knock sounds at her door.

"Come in," she says, closing the file as he steps inside. That's the first thing she notices about him now: the way he walks. He's deft, quiet. His physicality is twice what it was.

"Dr. Russo," Justin says, and she smiles as she meets those grateful blue eyes. Serena wonders if that's how he looks at the encantado; she can understand how he draws women in. "Thank you for seeing me."

"It's not me who deserves thanks." She gestures for him to sit in the chair across my desk. "I heard what you did in the forest."

He sits. "The other cadets were there, too."

"Of course. Tell me, how have you been feeling?"

"Since last night?"

"That, and since the procedure." She lifts a notepad and pen. "Like

I said, we want to know exactly how it's affecting you—for better and worse."

He sits back in the chair, his forearms flexing as he grips the armrests. "Well, it's mostly been for the better."

"But?"

"Well …" He hesitates. "There have been a few side effects."

Serena lifts her pen. "Tell me," she says. And because Justin Truly trusts her, he tells her everything she wants to know.

ALSO BY RAMY VANCE

Mortality Bites Series

Mortality Bites

Family Matters

Superhero Me!

Orphaned Follies

Dawn of a Thousand Sunsets

Three Dead Gods

Run, Kat, Run

Encantado Dreams

The Heaviest of Burdens

Looking for a great deal? Grab these book bundles...

Setting Fires with Dragons - complete series

Mortality Bound - complete series

GoneGod World - Complete series

Series Starter - Bundle

www.ingramcontent.com/pod-product-compliance
Lightning Source LLC
Chambersburg PA
CBHW030334030726
47499CB00003B/774